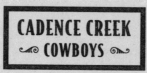

CADENCE CREEK
∽ COWBOYS ∽

They're the rough Diamonds of the West....

The cowboys of Cadence Creek have trouble as their
middle name. With chips on their shoulders the size
of hay bales, these rough and rugged men think they
need a woman the way they need a lame horse.
Little do they know…

Don't miss any of the action in Cadence Creek!

THE LAST REAL COWBOY
May 2012

THE REBEL RANCHER
June 2012

LITTLE COWGIRL ON HIS DOORSTEP
March 2013

A COWBOY TO COME HOME TO
July 2013

Dear Reader,

Do you remember your first love? Maybe not even your first real love, but that secret someone who made your heart beat faster, who made it difficult for you to breathe whenever they were around? What if that person was also your best friend? It would complicate things, wouldn't it?

When I started this book I knew that Cooper and Melissa had had a past. They'd never been a couple, but she'd had a real crush on him when she was younger. But he'd also been her best friend, and she'd finally had to let go of her romantic notions and accept that he'd always just be…a friend. She'd moved on—without knowing that Coop's feelings had changed.

Now they're all grown up, and old feelings are back. More than just old feelings, really, because they're not teenagers anymore. They're older, wiser, not thinking so much about stealing a kiss behind the bleachers but about failed marriages and old wounds and how risky it is to give your heart to someone.

There was something really special about writing this story, and I think it was that Coop and Mel had always had a connection that went deeper than friendship or attraction. They had a past that connected their hearts in a way that time couldn't erase.

I do hope you enjoy this latest Cadence Creek story—because I've certainly enjoyed exploring the town and the people who call it home. Come on in and make yourself at home. I've got a story to tell you….

Love,

Donna

DONNA ALWARD

A Cowboy To Come Home To

CADENCE CREEK
∽ COWBOYS ∽

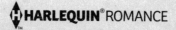

♦ HARLEQUIN® ROMANCE

Recycling programs
for this product may
not exist in your area.

ISBN-13: 978-0-373-74248-6

A COWBOY TO COME HOME TO

First North American Publication 2013

Copyright © 2013 by Donna Alward

⊕ HARLEQUIN®

Printed in U.S.A.

™ www.Harlequin.com

A busy wife and mother of three (two daughters and the family dog), **Donna Alward** believes hers is the best job in the world: a combination of stay-at-home mum and romance novelist. An avid reader since childhood, Donna always made up her own stories. She completed her arts degree in English literature in 1994, but it wasn't until 2001 that she penned her first full-length novel and found herself hooked on writing romance. In 2006 she sold her first manuscript, and now writes warm, emotional stories for the Harlequin® Romance line.

In her new home office in Nova Scotia, Donna loves being back on the east coast of Canada after nearly twelve years in Alberta, where her career began, writing about cowboys and the West. Donna's debut romance, *Hired by the Cowboy,* was awarded the Bookseller's Best Award in 2008 for Best Traditional Romance.

With the Atlantic Ocean only minutes from her doorstep, Donna has found a fresh take on life and promises even more great romances in the near future!

Donna loves to hear from readers. You can contact her through her website, www.donnaalward.com, her page at www.myspace.com/dalward, or through her publisher.

Recent books by Donna Alward

LITTLE COWGIRL ON HIS DOORSTEP *
SLEIGH RIDE WITH THE RANCHER
THE REBEL RANCHER *
THE LAST REAL COWBOY *
HOW A COWBOY STOLE HER HEART
A FAMILY FOR THE RUGGED RANCHER
HONEYMOON WITH THE RANCHER

*Cadence Creek Cowboys

Other titles by this author available in ebook format.

CHAPTER ONE

COOPER FORD WAS six foot two of faded denim and plaid cotton, accessorized by an insufferable ego.

The smile slid off of Melissa Stone's face as Coop pulled the door to the flower shop closed behind him, the little brass bell dinging annoyingly as he reached up and took off his hat. Oh, wasn't he all charm and politeness. Melissa's replacement smile was plastic and somewhat forced. Just what she needed at five o'clock on a Friday afternoon. To be face-to-face with the one man left in Cadence Creek who she wished would simply dry up and blow away.

"Afternoon, Melissa."

She gritted her teeth at the sound of his deep voice, somehow musical even when saying the most mundane things. "Cooper."

She refused to call him Coop like everyone else in town. Like she had years ago when they'd all hung out together, having a few beers around a campfire after a Sunday-night softball game. When he'd been the sort of guy she'd been proud to call *friend*. Now he was Cooper. If she thought he'd let her get away with it, she'd call him Mr. Ford. He deserved it.

But that would be a little *too* obvious. A very stiff "Cooper" sent the same message with a touch more subtlety—even if he did remain Coop in her head. The old days were gone. They weren't friends any longer. To her recollection, this was the first time he'd ever deigned to darken the flower shop door.

He smiled at her. "Nice day out there. Cool, but sunny."

Oh, this was positively painful. The weather? Seriously? She blinked, trying to ignore Coop's big frame, which fit perfectly into his dusty jeans and the worn denim jacket that looked as if he'd had it for at least a decade. The edges of the collar and cuffs were white and slightly frayed. The jacket gaped open, revealing an old plaid shirt with a streak of dirt smeared across his chest.

One positive thing she could say about Coop: he wasn't lazy. From the look of him he was straight off the ranch. From the smell of him, too—the pungent but not unpleasant scent of horses clung to his clothing.

"Forecast says frost maybe tonight." She resisted the urge to tap her nails on the counter. The weather, she realized, was a safe topic. "What can I do for you, Cooper?"

He bumped his hat on the side of his leg. "I need some flowers."

His gaze dropped to the green apron she wore when she was in her shop. The words Foothills Floral Design were embroidered on the left breast. Pockets lined the bottom, where she could keep her scissors and pocket knife and anything else she needed as she worked around the store.

Her cheeks heated. No big surprise that Cooper was staring at her breasts. He liked women, did Cooper Ford. When she'd been married, Coop had a new girl hanging off his arm every other month, it seemed. A real love-'em-and-leave-'em kind of guy. She took a deep breath. "What kind of flowers?"

His gaze lifted to meet hers and she found herself drawn to the golden flecks in the hazel depths. He had lashes that were too long to be decent for any self-respecting man, which made his eyes quite pretty.

Pretty enough for him to get away with just about anything in this town, she reminded herself with disgust. Except with her. She knew exactly what kind of guy Cooper was. He'd definitely shown his true colors the day he'd betrayed their friendship.

"I don't know," he confessed with a sheepish grin. "Something big. Something that says I'm really, really sorry."

Acid soured her stomach. Ugh. Apology flowers. And she could just imagine what the combo of Coop and a big bouquet would do to some silly doe-eyed girl who didn't know any better. "Who'd you do wrong now, Coop?"

The words were out before she could think better of them and she couldn't take them back.

His gaze sharpened, but he merely raised one eyebrow. It made her feel small, as she always did when she was reminded of what a fool she'd been three years ago.

Walking in on her husband, Scott, and his girlfriend had been the most humiliating moment of her life. It had made her one big cliché.

She'd thought it couldn't get any worse, but then she'd discovered that Coop had known all along. He'd been aware that her husband—his best buddy—was having an affair. And he hadn't said a single, blessed word to her about it. No heads-up. No…nothing.

The joke had totally been on her, and she'd never forgotten it. Even now, as she took the steps to truly move on—alone—his betrayal stung. There was sticking by your friend and there was doing what was right. Cooper didn't choose right.

"I missed my mother's birthday," he replied, putting his weight on one hip and hooking a thumb in his jeans pocket. "I was out of town all week. But it was her sixtieth and so now I'm trying to make it up to her."

Once more Melissa felt foolish. She didn't like Cooper. Actually, the truth was more that she didn't trust him. She didn't respect him. She should just let it go, like water off a duck's back, as the old saying went. She definitely should not let him get to her, especially after all this time.

"Oh," she answered. "Then I'm sure I can help. Do you want it in a vase or paper?"

"Paper," he answered. "She's got a million vases around the house. And no roses. They're too formal and old-ladyish. Something mixed."

Melissa tended to agree. Not that roses weren't great, and they were definitely a classic—elegant and timeless. But she secretly preferred something simpler, more wildflowerish and whimsical. "Colors?"

"Yellows. Maybe with some red and blue in it? Colorful and, well, large. It's a big apology."

He smiled down at Melissa and she nearly

smiled back before catching herself. "Give me fifteen minutes or so," she replied, jotting the order on her notepad. "You can come back and pick it up, yeah?"

He nodded. "It'll give me time to go to the pharmacy and get a nice card."

"Gee, nothing says 'Happy Birthday, Mom' like a last-minute card," she replied drily.

He didn't answer.

"Okay," she said, putting down her pen. "Fifteen minutes."

"Thanks, Mel," he said, putting his hat back on his head.

Mel.

No one had called her that in ages. Certainly not Cooper, who she avoided as often as possible, which took some creativity in a town the size of Cadence Creek. Thankfully, he felt the same way, and even if they ended up at the same functions, they steered well clear of each other. Opposite ends of the room sort of thing. Definitely no eye contact or chitchat.

But hearing the shortened version of her name—Mel—took her back to the old days. The days when she'd thought she was happy, and she'd really been living in a fantasy world.

The bell chimed as he left, a cheerful sound that was out of key with her current dismal mood, a good portion of which had nothing to do with Cooper at all. She was getting tired of taking her temperature every darn day. Of getting her hopes up, only to be faced with disappointment. Of spending her savings on trying to get pregnant the nontraditional way. She was going to give it one more try, but she wasn't holding out a lot of hope. Maybe she'd be better off filling out the paperwork for the adoption registry.

But deep down, she wasn't ready to give up. The end of her marriage had also marked the end of her plans for a brilliant life. Plans that had included starting a family. Why should she give that up just because circumstances had changed? She'd done so many things on her own since the divorce, like start her own successful business. She was absolutely certain she could manage this, too.

She would be a good mom if given the chance.

But first she had to look after Cooper's order. She was just getting out the red gerbera daisies when Penny arrived for her Friday-night shift. Penny was in eleventh grade at the high school and was the best worker Melissa had on staff. Most of the time she wished she could have her for more shifts, but Penny and her parents were firm on the eight-hours-a-week rule. Melissa got her Friday from five to nine and Saturday morning from nine to one and that was it.

Melissa hoped that if the planets aligned and things finally went right, she could offer Penny a lot more hours next summer—especially if Melissa was spending more time at home with a baby. Between Penny and Amy Wilkins, who covered a lot of the day shifts, Melissa had some breathing room in the schedule.

Penny's arrival meant Melissa wouldn't have to wait on Cooper when he returned. All she had to do was finish making up the arrangement before he came back.

Her fingers plucked bright yellow yarrow a little quicker at the prospect. Cooper Ford had nothing to do with her current life.

She made her own way now, and that was exactly how it was going to stay.

Cooper let out a breath when he was out on the sidewalk again. He'd finally gathered up the courage to go into her shop. This nonsense of avoiding each other had gone on long enough. Surely after three years she might have mellowed where he was concerned.

But nothing had changed, had it? Melissa still looked at him as if he were dirt beneath her heel. It had been a long time since she and Scott had split. But the truth was she still hated Scott, and she still hated Cooper's guts because he'd known about the affair and hadn't said a word.

He walked away from the flower shop, his long legs eating up the concrete as he made his way to the drugstore. The problem with Melissa was that she didn't know the whole story. She thought Cooper had kept his mouth shut because he'd been looking out for his best buddy. "Their little club," she'd called it. And she'd called him a lot more than that, too, words he would never have imagined coming out of that sweet little mouth. He'd taken all the verbal slings because she'd been right. Not in her interpretation of how it all went down, and definitely not right about his motives. But she'd been right that he should have had the guts to say something. God knows he wanted to. He'd come close so many times....

But all his life he'd been a coward where Melissa was concerned, and the day she'd walked in on Scott with another woman hadn't changed anything. Cooper had had no right to her friendship after that. He'd failed her, and she would never know how badly he felt about it.

At the drugstore, he headed for the greeting card aisle. Without too much trouble he picked out a birthday card for his mother, but he paused as he passed by a smaller section of cards. Close to the thank-you notes were half a dozen with I'm Sorry messages on the fronts. They sported sappy pictures of flowers and cute puppies and kittens. He gave a dry chuckle as he picked one up and opened the flap. There were no words on the inside, just a blank space to write in a personal message.

He imagined what he'd write to Melissa. "I'm sorry for keeping the truth from you all those years ago," maybe? It was true. But it wouldn't be enough. Not for her. And there was no way in hell he was going to write "I'm sorry I didn't tell you about your husband's infidelity, but I was in love with you and didn't want to hurt you."

Even if he were stupid enough to confess such a thing, it didn't even scrape the surface of what had really happened.

He'd been between a rock and a hard place and it had marked the end of his lifelong friendship with Scott. Not that that mattered one bit to Melissa, he thought bitterly. Not once had she considered how he might be caught in the middle, between his two best friends.

He put the card back in the slot and went to the cash register. Once outside, he headed back to the flower shop, gearing himself up for another few minutes of pretending they didn't have any past history at all.

But when he went back inside Foothills Floral, there was no sign of Melissa. Instead, a teenager with braces smiled at him and rang up his purchase.

He left and got into his truck, a crease forming between his brows.

It appeared he wasn't the only coward.

The early September sky was the clear, deep blue that Melissa particularly loved, and it seemed to go on forever. As she got out of her car and shut the door, she took a deep, restorative breath. How she loved this time of year. Everything was warm and mellow after the brash heat of summer. The prairie was green and golden, the air crisp and the leaves on the poplars and birches were turning a stunning golden yellow. It reminded her of back-to-school days and how she'd loved filling up her new backpack and lunch bag and getting on the school bus as a girl. It reminded her of sitting on the bleachers during football season, cheering on the Cadence Creek Cougars and, in particular, Scott.

Well, that memory was a little tainted now, but she still remembered what it had been like to be nearly seventeen and in love with the handsome star of the team.

These days the fall weather made her want to

do all sorts of nesting things, like baking and freezing and canning and knitting. It was silly, because why would she bother freezing and canning for herself? Maybe if she had a family, a few kids running around...

She shook her head and focused on the house in front of her. She had a good life. Maybe it hadn't turned out exactly as she'd planned, but she had a thriving business and a nice, if small, home. She had good friends and a lot to be thankful for.

She looked up at the unfinished structure before her. Things could definitely be worse. Take, for instance, Stu Dickinson and his family. They were going to own this house when it was finished. The Dickinsons had been living in a cheap duplex rental in town when it had burned and they'd lost everything. With his wife suffering from multiple sclerosis and unable to work, Stu was the sole breadwinner for them and their two kids. Tenant's insurance had made it possible for them to replace necessities, but they were struggling to make ends meet.

Which was where a local charity organization came in.

Melissa wasn't that great with power tools, but she'd signed up to volunteer now that the house was framed. She had no idea what she'd be doing today, but the coordinator had assured her that she'd be fine and that someone would show her exactly what to do.

When she stepped inside the house, the racket was unbelievable. The shrill whine of a saw rang in her ears, followed by a bang and the sound of male voices.

"Hello?" she called out in a brief moment of silence, putting her purse by the door. The room on her left had been finished with Sheetrock and had had its cracks filled, but not painted. The one on the right was still only framed and the wiring was visible, including electrical outlets and dangling wires for an overhead light fixture.

Boots sounded at the back of the house and she wiped her hands on her jeans. "Hello?" a voice returned.

A strange feeling slithered through her stomach in the instant before the man appeared.

"You!" she exclaimed. Oh, wasn't this just her luck! Twice in one week, no less.

Cooper halted in the doorway to the hall. "Oh," he answered, his face going completely blank for the space of a second. "You're volunteering today?"

She nodded. He sounded as pleased about it as she was. "And I take it you are, too?"

He nodded in turn.

She couldn't back out now. For one, she'd committed to volunteering. And two, if she did withdraw, Cooper would know it was all because of him. She wouldn't give him the satisfaction.

At some point it might be good if they could be in the same room together without her wanting to spit in his eye.

He took off his gloves. "Stu works for me. Least I can do is help out, you know?"

Melissa blinked. "I would have thought things were too busy out at your place." Cooper's ranch was profitable and his reputation for breeding great stock horses was growing. Ranchers from all over the prairies and northern states came to the Double C for their cutting and working horses.

"Sure it's busy. But I don't run it alone. I have good men working for me. They know what they're doing and I trust them. You know what it's like. You must have someone working the shop this morning."

She did. Against her better judgment she'd hired Amy Wilkins on a part-time basis. Amy's reputation around town wasn't always the greatest, but Melissa had taken a chance and given the vivacious blonde a try. So far she'd worked out well. She was a fast learner and was good with the customers. The only thing she couldn't do was arrange flowers, so Melissa had gone in early to do up the day's orders and make sure the cooler was filled with prearranged bouquets for walk-in sales.

"So, is there someone here to tell me what I need to do?"

Cooper grinned. "Yep. Me, for now. The bedrooms are all painted, and we've just finished laying the floor in the master. How are you with a brad nailer? We've got the baseboard and crown molding ready to go."

Melissa hesitated. Couldn't he install the trim while she worked with someone else? The last thing she wanted was to spend the next four hours in the same room with Coop.

"Melissa."

His rough voice pulled her back. "What?"

"Is it so bad? Really?"

She met his gaze. He wasn't smiling, wasn't making fun or trying to be charming—for once. He was dead serious. He shifted his gloves from one hand to the other—was he nervous? He hadn't aged, other than a few lines in the corners of his eyes that were more likely from the sun and wind than time passing. He still looked so much like the boy she'd laughed with over the years. Though she wouldn't admit it out loud in a thousand years, she missed that guy. Once upon a time she'd called him her best friend.

"You remind me," she said coolly. "You remind me, okay? Of how stupid and naive I once was."

"I'm sorry about that." He took a step forward. "But I can't change it. We're grown-ups. Surely we can manage to work together for a few hours without killing each other."

He was right. "Yeah, well, this place isn't about you or me, so we just have to suck it up, right? Besides, I don't know much about construction, so it appears I get to swallow my pride and let you boss me around."

He smiled then, a crooked upturn of his lips that reached his eyes. "Like I could ever tell you what to do."

The air hummed between them for a few minutes. Briefly, Melissa missed the way things used to be, the easy rapport they had shared. Cooper had been a tease, though she'd always known that his flirting meant nothing. It had been safe to banter back and forth because he was Scott's best friend as well as hers. He'd given the toast at their wedding, for Pete's sake.

She ignored his last statement and checked her watch. "Shouldn't we get started? I only have until one o'clock, when I have to be back at the shop."

He led the way to the master bedroom, pausing briefly to introduce her to the other people working there, installing oak hardwood in the other bedrooms. To her surprise she saw Callum Shepard, a local dairy farmer and newcomer to town, and Rhys Bullock, Martha Bullock's son and one of the hands over at Diamondback Ranch. The big surprise was that they were being bossed around by Chelsea Smith, whose father owned the hardware store.

After the hellos, Melissa followed Cooper to the back bedroom, pausing in the doorway to admire what had already been done. The walls were the shade of her favorite vanilla latte, and the rich color of the hardwood looked lovely against it. There were windows in two walls, providing a view of the distant Rockies in one direction and a view of the creek valley that ran to the north in the other.

"This is nice," she said, stepping in and hearing her boots echo on the wood floor.

"Stu deserves it. They were already struggling to make ends meet, and then to lose all their belongings… Sometimes life just isn't fair. I'm glad they were able to get this going and

I'm happy to help. He's a good man and a good worker. He deserved a break."

It was easier to dismiss Coop when he was being deliberately charming. When he was sincere it was hard to remember why she resented him so much.

Lengths of baseboard were stretched across the floor, and a saw was set up on a heavy drop cloth. A loud drone filled the room as the air compressor fired up.

Cooper saw to filling the air nailer and then reached for his measuring tape. "Hold this here," he commanded, leaving her with one end. Together they measured the wall, then measured the baseboard—twice—and Cooper marked it with a carpenter's pencil.

She held the end while he made the first cut, then angled the other side with the miter saw so the next piece would match up in the corner.

Together they moved the piece to the wall, putting it flush against the end cap of the woodwork in the doorway. "Okay, now you're on. I'll hold it in place and you nail it."

"Me?"

"Sure, you. Take the nailer and press it against that hollow part there." He pointed to the curve in the baseboard design. "Is it pressed all the way in? Okay, now squeeze the trigger."

With a loud snap, the nailer jerked in her hand. "Is that right?"

"Looks good to me. Keep going."

The tool felt odd in her hand, and the noise was loud, especially when the compressor kicked in again. But it was kind of fun, nailing the molding into place. They had to adjust a cut when working their way around the doorway for the walk-in closet, but for the moment Melissa forgot about how much she disliked Cooper, and simply focused on the job.

They worked in relative silence as they finished the baseboard, and then moved on to the crown molding. This was harder, getting the angle just right. It took a few tries with each piece, and nailing it in place was awkward when Melissa had to hold the nailer above her head.

It was after twelve when they finished. She stood back as Cooper took a tube of wood filler and touched up the corner seams where there were inevitable tiny gaps. He took his time and she watched him on the stepladder, the way his jeans fit and how his customary cotton plaid shirt spread across broad, muscled shoulders. Scott hadn't been the only one on the football and hockey teams. Cooper had been a bit of a jock, too. But unlike Scott, he'd never had a girl watching from the stands.

Nope, he'd had about ten girls, all gazing at him with love-struck expressions, sighing blissfully if he ever turned his attention to them. Which he did. Just never for too long. And never at Melissa.

"Once this is dry, it'll just need to be touched up with a bit of paint. What do you think?"

Melissa looked away so he wouldn't know she'd been staring at him, and made a point of sweeping her gaze around the room. "It looks finished," she said, realizing it truly did. "The crown molding was a nice touch."

"We didn't do that in the kids' rooms," Cooper said, screwing the cap back on the tube. "It's expensive. It's a nice addition in here, though."

Melissa checked her watch. "My time's just about up. Are you done here, too?"

Cooper nodded. "For today. I come out most mornings for a couple of hours and lend a hand. Bring the guys coffee. It won't be long now until it's ready. The drywall guy is coming back tomorrow to finish the den, and then it's just painting the front rooms, putting down the flooring and installing the kitchen cupboards. You coming back another day?"

He rolled up the hose from the compressor as he spoke. Melissa paused. It hadn't been so bad, being with Cooper. Awkward and at times uncomfortable, but they'd been civil, which was more than they'd accomplished in years.

Now that she'd seen the house and helped it take shape, even just a little, she wanted to come back and help out again. "I'll have to check the work schedule at the shop and call the coordinator. Amy's fine with running the store, but I'm the only floral designer."

"Well, there's always stuff to be done. I'm sure your help would be welcomed."

On the way out of the house Melissa stopped and picked up her purse. Cooper had put the compressor in the hall by the other bedrooms and she heard his voice as he spoke to some workers. She was walking to her car when he called out her name.

She turned and saw him jogging her way. "Hey," he said, slowing as he approached. "I'm going to pick up the lunch order from the Wagon Wheel and bring it back. You want to grab a sandwich or something?"

With him? There was letting bygones be bygones and then there was…what? Lunch for two at the busiest spot in town? They'd been civil this week, but the idea of sitting down and making pleasant conversation was unfathomable. They weren't *friends*. Adults, maybe, but the time for friendship and hanging out together was long gone. It was far too late to rewrite the past.

"I have to get back to the shop, sorry," she stated, reaching into her purse for her keys.

Cooper stood back. "Sure. Maybe another time," he suggested, though they both knew it wasn't really an invitation.

"Maybe," she agreed, but it was an empty agreement.

"See you around, Mel."

"Yeah. Bye, Coop."

She reached for the door handle and scooted behind the wheel before he could see the color rise in her cheeks.

She'd called him Coop. After staring at his behind and being asked out to lunch.

This was exactly why she had said no. The last thing she needed in her life was a complication like Cooper Ford. They'd done a good job of avoiding each other in the past, and she could take care to do it again.

CHAPTER TWO

SHE MANAGED TO AVOID HIM for almost two weeks.

Melissa yawned and locked the door to the shop. Saturdays and most weeknights she closed at six, except for Fridays, when she stayed open until nine. Last night had been crazy busy with walk-in traffic, which had been unusual but good. And today she'd had to interrupt her design time to help Penny cover the front. People were purchasing fall arrangements, particularly sunflowers and warm-colored mums and zinnias. Premade silk wreaths for front doors were disappearing like hotcakes and so were decorative sheaves of wheat.

To top it off, she'd barely finished the weekly standing order of flowers for the church when the president of the Ladies' Circle had come to pick it up. And Melissa had moved directly from that to working on the arrangement for a funeral happening on Monday.

Now orders were flooding in for the funeral

home, and instead of taking a day off on Sunday, she knew she was going to be spending her one lazy day a week here at work, rather than at home vacuuming and doing laundry.

She loved the store and owning her own business, but there were downsides, too.

She'd walked to work this morning, taking the extra precious minutes to enjoy the cool air and fall sunshine. Now she wished she'd brought her car. All she really wanted was a quick dinner and a hot bath before falling into bed.

She'd take care of the quick dinner by stopping at the diner, she decided. The sunlight was fading as she made her way down Main Street and around the corner to the busy restaurant. The parking lot was full and she nearly considered just going home and ordering a pizza. But the great thing about the diner was the convenience of a restaurant with the advantage of good home cooking. When she stepped inside and saw that the special was meat loaf and mashed potatoes, she was sold. Total comfort food.

She placed her order and waited just beyond the counter.

The noise was deafening and she closed her eyes, reminding herself that it was only a few minutes and she could find peace and quiet at home.

And then there was a warm hand on her shoulder and a deep voice said, "Mel, are you okay?"

She opened her eyes to find Cooper's worried ones staring down at her. For a split second something exciting leaped at the recognition of his fingers gripping her shoulder. Embarrassed, she nodded quickly, slipping away from his touch. "Fine. I'm just waiting for my order."

"With your eyes closed?"

She shrugged, even though she felt ridiculous. "I'm tired and it's loud. That's all."

"Melissa? Your order's up," Martha Bullock called out from behind the counter, holding up a white paper bag.

Relieved, Melissa stepped forward to collect it, only to hear Martha announce, "Yours, too, Coop. Extra cheese and a side order of onion rings, just like you wanted."

He took the bag from Martha and handed her a twenty, then leaned forward and kissed the older woman's cheek. "You sure know how to look after a man," he teased, sending her a wink.

"Oh, go on with you," she answered, flapping a hand at him but grinning widely. "Your charm's wasted on me."

"Did you put in extra ketchup?"

"Sure I did."

"Then it's not wasted. Have a good night, Martha."

Melissa restrained herself from rolling her eyes. The thing about Cooper was that the teasing truly was genuine. He was a charmer, but there wasn't anything fake about it. If there had been, people would see clear through it. Maybe that was what had hurt so much. Coop had been the most honest, genuine man she'd ever known. Until, of course, he'd lied.

It was quieter outside. Melissa expelled a huge breath. "Well, good night." She started walking across the parking lot to the sidewalk.

Cooper's voice stopped her. "Hey, Mel, you want a lift? Getting dark for you to be walking home alone."

"I'll be fine. I like the air."

"But my truck's right here. I can drop you off, no trouble."

She halted and turned back, pasting on a smile. She did not want Cooper Ford driving her home or anywhere else. "Really," she said firmly. "I'll be fine."

He frowned. He was wearing the same battered jean jacket as he had that day in her shop, and she marveled once more at how broad his shoulders were. She should not be noticing these things. She wasn't exactly blind, she reminded herself, but the real problem was they shouldn't matter. She couldn't honestly say they were simple detached observations. She noticed, and then she got this odd feeling. Kind of tingly and warm.

"If you won't take a drive, I'll walk you home."

Suddenly he didn't seem so attractive. Why did he have to be all up in her business lately? Hadn't they managed to avoid each other quite successfully the past three years? It had been an unspoken agreement, and suddenly he was breaking it left, right and center.

She decided to ask. While the smell of meat loaf wafted up and teased her nostrils, she squared her shoulders and faced him. "Why now, Cooper? For three years we've barely said two words to each other. Now all of a sudden you're making conversation and offering to walk me home—in Cadence Creek, and on a route I've walked a million times."

He stepped closer. "How long did you think we could each pretend that the other didn't exist? I guess I thought three years was enough time for you to stop hating me quite so much. That we could stop avoiding each other in a town this small. It's gotten to be quite a challenge, you know. Trying to stay out of your way."

"I don't hate you."

"Really?"

He raised his eyebrow again, and she could practically hear what he was silently saying. *Riiight.*

She sighed. "You're not going to just let me go home, are you?"

"Not walking alone. Cadence Creek is a nice town, but it's not totally crime free, you know. Stuff happens."

"Fine. But I'm still walking. I need the fresh air. It's been a long day."

He caught up to her and fell into step beside her on the sidewalk. "I haven't seen you at the house this week."

"I was there one afternoon and did some painting in the living room. You were gone already when I arrived."

"I'm sure you planned it that way."

She kept walking. It was kind of surreal, strolling through town in the semidark with Cooper. "I ended up being swamped this week," she confessed. "If this keeps up, I'm going to have to hire a part-time designer."

She bit down on her lip. She'd also made a trip to Edmonton, to the clinic, when conditions were "right." A few weeks from now she'd know whether or not she needed to pee on a stick. She kept telling herself not to get her hopes up, but each morning when she woke, the first thing she thought of was that this time next year she could be a mother.

They were passing by the Creekside Park and Playground when Cooper reached out and put his hand on her arm. "Hey, why don't we stop and eat? There are a few picnic tables here, and our food's getting cold."

"You want to eat in the dark? Are you crazy?"

"By the time I walk you home and get back to my truck, my stuff will be cold."

"You didn't have to walk me," she pointed out.

"Yes, I did."

She recognized that tone. Cooper was charm itself, but he was also incredibly stubborn. Not only that, but she was so hungry her stomach was actually hurting, and the food smelled unbelievable. "Fine. You're going to pester me until you get your way, anyway."

They crossed the grass to a picnic table and Melissa spread out the paper bag as a place mat. Cooper took the spot across from her and began pulling take-out containers from his own bag. She gaped as she counted three: an extra-large one holding his burger and fries, a medium-sized one with onion rings that smelled fantastic and a smaller one with the Wagon Wheel's special recipe coleslaw.

"You're going to eat all of that? Yourself?"

"I'm a growing boy." He patted his flat belly and opened the container holding his burger.

She shook her head. "It's a wonder you're not the size of a barn."

She picked up her plastic fork and dipped it into the mashed potatoes and gravy. The food wasn't piping-hot any longer, but was still quite warm, and as she tasted the first bite she was struck by a pang so bittersweet it made her heart ache.

This was something they might have done in the old days: a bunch of them together, some takeout, hanging out on a Saturday night. Only it wasn't a bunch anymore, but just she and Cooper. Some of their circle of friends had drifted away, some had left Cadence Creek and gone to work in bigger towns and cities. So little of the past remained. In some ways it was good, but in other ways, Melissa missed it. Up until things had blown apart, there'd been a lot of good times.

"You okay?" Cooper asked, pausing to look at her while holding a French fry.

"Yeah, I'm fine. Just thinking about when we were kids, and some of the stuff we used to do on a Saturday night. It sure wasn't picking up takeout because we were too tired from dealing with 'real life' to cook."

He chuckled. "We all have to grow up some-time. At least mostly."

He held out the box of onion rings. "Have one. You know you want to."

She wasn't sure if she was glad that he re-membered her fondness for onion rings or not. It was too much to resist as he waved them under her nose. She reached into the package and took out a round battered ring. When she bit into it, her teeth caught the onion and it came out of the batter. She pulled it into her mouth like a piece of spaghetti.

Cooper laughed. "Good, right?"

"So good," she admitted.

He put the box between them on the table, an unspoken invitation to share. A peace offering? Was he hoping that the deep-fried treat would accomplish what time had not? It was a big thing to ask from a carton of onion rings.

For the moment, she chose to cut into her meat loaf and peas and carrots.

They were quiet for a few minutes, eating and listening to the breeze whisper through the leaves that still remained on the poplars lining the creek. She didn't know what to say to him. Talking about the past would only bring up the painful way her marriage had broken apart. And anything else seemed…contrived. Awkward. He ate his burger in silence as she finished her meal, then he handed her another onion ring before taking one for himself and dipping it in ketchup.

"You still like doing that?" she commented.

"Yeah. Ketchup should be a food group all by itself." He put his empty containers in his bag. She did the same with hers and they left the picnic table, stopping at the garbage cans to deposit their waste.

"Feel better?" he asked quietly.

She did, surprisingly. It wasn't just the food, either, although she'd been very hungry. She'd had a few moments to breathe, to unwind. Funny how he'd seemed to know she'd needed that. Or maybe she was reading too much into his motives. Maybe it truly was all about eating his dinner while it was hot.

"I do feel better," she admitted. "I was pretty spooled up after my day."

"Give me five more minutes, okay? Come with me."

She frowned but followed. He led her over to the swings. "Sit down."

"Okay, now you're being silly. I just want to go home and get off my feet."

In response, he sat on the swing beside hers.

It was set low for kids, and his long legs folded up like a frog's, but he pushed off anyway and put it in motion. "This gets you off your feet. Look." He held his booted feet up in the air. He looked ridiculous.

She felt foolish, but sat down and scuffed one shoe in the dirt, making the swing rock a little.

"Hold on to the chains and lean back."

"Cooper, you're crazy."

"Do it, Mel. Lean back and then open your eyes."

She pushed with her foot a little harder, then gripped the chains between her fingers and leaned back. The breeze from the motion ruffled her hair, making bits of it feather across her cheeks. Slowly, she opened her eyes and looked up.

There were stars. Not too many, but a handful that seemed to rock in the sky as she swayed back and forth. When had they come out? Sometime between leaving the restaurant and eating her dinner in the twilight.

The sky was so big, so endless. She heard a loud sigh and realized it had come from herself. As she watched, more stars appeared out of nowhere. One second vast emptiness, then the next time she looked, *pop.* There they were, twinkling down at her from the infinite blackness.

"Make a wish," Cooper suggested.

Her throat tightened. What in the world was she doing, sitting on the swings in the dark with Cooper Ford? "I'm too old for that nonsense. Besides, that's for the first star you see, and there are at least two dozen right now."

His voice was low and warm beside her. "Then make two dozen wishes. Wish on every one."

"Cooper…"

She knew it was stupid and juvenile, but she couldn't resist. She closed her eyes and made a wish.

Let this time be the one.

All she really wanted was to be a mom. She'd wanted it when she was married to Scott, and they'd supposedly been trying when she'd caught him cheating. The divorce had killed not only their marriage but her dream of a family, too. And she wasn't interested in getting married again.

But the longing for a family, for a child of her own, hadn't abated. If she could survive starting her own business and her marriage blowing up, she could handle being a single mom. She certainly didn't want to marry someone she didn't love just to make that happen. That made less sense than doing it alone.

She really wanted the pregnancy to take this time. If not, she could look into adoption, but she truly wanted to experience the joy of carrying her baby inside her. There was just something so…complete about it.

"You still here, or are you on another planet?"

Coop's voice intruded. Her swing had stopped swaying and her arms were twined around the chains, while her face remained tilted toward the sky. She swallowed and opened her eyes. "I'm still here. It takes a while to make twenty-four wishes."

He chuckled in the darkness. That funny curling sensation wound its way through her stomach again.

She jumped off the swing and brushed her hands down her trousers. "I really do need to get home. I've got to be back to work tomorrow to do up all the arrangements for the Madison funeral."

"All work and no play makes Mel a dull girl."

She shrugged and reached for her purse. "It happens when you own your own business. You know how it is. There's no real time clock to punch."

"Yeah, I know. I'm going to be locked up in my office tomorrow going over paperwork."

They made their way back to the sidewalk

and on toward Melissa's house. "We really did grow up, didn't we, Cooper?"

His boots sounded on the concrete, steady thumps that seemed slightly out of place and yet reassuring. "Yes, we did. And some of it was painful."

Melissa had hoped he wasn't going to bring it up. She shivered in the rapidly cooling air. Without saying a word, Coop took off his jean jacket and slid it over her shoulders.

"Live and learn." She injected some lightness into her voice, as if it was no big deal.

Her house was just a few blocks away now. She had to put him off for only a minute or so and she'd be home and he'd be gone.

"Live and learn?" Coop stopped and put a hand on her arm, halting her, too. His voice was harsh. "You don't talk to me for three years and then come out with a flippant 'live and learn'?"

She pulled her arm away from his fingers. That was twice tonight he'd taken the liberty of touching her. "Maybe you should take the hint that I don't want to talk about it."

They carried on for a few minutes, the silence growing increasingly awkward between them. Twenty more steps and she'd be at her front walk. She was nearly there when she realized she couldn't hear his boots just behind her anymore. For some weird reason her heart was pounding, but she made herself keep going. She took five more steps before his voice stopped her.

"I was wrong."

She slowed, paused for just a breath of a moment, but kept walking. They weren't going to do this. Not tonight and not on the sidewalk outside her house.

The memory of their argument was still fresh in her mind—as if it had happened yesterday—and nearly as painful. She'd been so angry at Scott. Angry and hurt with the vitriolic bitterness of a wife betrayed. But with Coop, it had been different. It had been a trust of a different kind that he'd broken. She'd been hurt by that, too. Hurt and disappointed that the one person she'd turned to when everything blew up had already known. He'd betrayed her, too.

"So you said already," she replied, wondering why the last twenty steps felt like a hundred.

"I thought maybe you'd be willing to accept my apology after all this time."

His longer legs caught up with her by the time she reached the first row of interlocking patio blocks that wound their way to her front door.

"Melissa. Please. Hasn't this gone on long enough?"

"What, our hating each other?"

She looked up into his face. In the glow of the streetlamp, he actually looked hurt. That was preposterous. She'd been the person wronged in all of this and they both knew it.

"I *never* hated you."

"Well, you sure never cared about me. That was clear enough."

A muscle ticked in his jaw and his gaze slid away for a moment. He took a deep breath and let it out before looking down into her eyes again.

She really wished he wouldn't do that. It was so hard to stay angry when he gazed at her that way, all wide eyes and long eyelashes. *"Bedroom eyes,"* her mother had said once. Eyes that were used to getting him what he wanted.

Melissa also knew she was entitled to her anger. Coop had told her once that he would always be there for her. And when push came to shove, he hadn't been. There was no way he could deny it.

"I never hated you," he insisted softly. "Not ever. It was complicated, but you are completely right in that I should have told you. I was wrong, Melissa, and I'm sorry. You have no idea how sorry."

She did not want to believe him or be touched by his apology. It was a real struggle, because he was looking at her so earnestly that she knew he wasn't lying. Nor was he trying to charm or joke his way out of anything.

But one thing stuck in her mind from that whole speech, and it wasn't that he'd admitted he was in the wrong, or that he was swallowing his pride to apologize.

It was that he'd said it was complicated.

"How complicated could it have been, Coop?" She kept her voice down—there were neighbors to consider—but her words were still crystal clear in the cool night. "Scott was cheating on me and you knew about it."

"Scott was my best friend."

"So was I. You said you'd always look out for me. You were like my big brother, do you know that?" She lifted her chin and finally said what she'd wanted to for ages. "You knew he was with her in the afternoon and coming home to me at night. Do you know how sick that is?" Tears pricked Melissa's eyes. "How dirty I felt for months afterward? All it would have taken was a few words from you. I trusted you, Coop."

He ran his hand over his hair. "Mel."

Her name sounded ragged coming from his lips. So he wasn't completely unaffected, either. Good.

"I trusted you," she repeated, softer now, and

a sadness took over where her anger had lived. Sadness and acceptance.

"I was friends with both of you. Have you even considered for one moment how caught in the middle I was? I swear, as soon as I found out I confronted him about it. I begged him to put a stop to it. I *demanded*."

"Did you threaten to tell me?"

"Yes."

"And yet you didn't."

He swallowed and looked away. "No."

"And why is that?"

He didn't answer, but they'd come this far and she wanted to know. He'd been the one to open the can of worms, and now he would have to deal with her questions. "Why didn't you tell me, if you told him you would?"

Cooper took a few moments to respond, and when he did his words seemed measured. "Scott said he would deny it, and that you'd believe him."

She frowned, puzzled. "Maybe I would *want* to believe him, but don't you think I'd ask why you would tell me such a thing if it wasn't true? Come on, Coop."

He shoved his hands into his pockets. "Look, my intention wasn't to relive this thing from start to finish, okay? I just wanted to say I was wrong, and that I'm sorry. Isn't it time we moved on?"

It bothered her that he was probably right. It had gone on a long time. She'd picked herself up and dusted herself off, made a good life for herself. The one thing she hadn't done was let go of her resentment for Cooper. Funny how she'd been able to put Scott in the past and not miss him a bit, but not Cooper. She supposed it came from staying in the same town and being faced with seeing him on a regular basis, even from a distance.

"I forgave you a long time ago, Coop."

"You could've fooled me."

"Forgiving isn't the same as forgetting. You're right. It's over and done. But you know the old saying, *Fool me once, shame on you, fool me twice...*'"

"'Shame on me'," he finished.

"Our friendship as it used to be is over, Cooper. We can't go back. It's how I'm built. Once someone hurts me, they don't get a chance to do it again. Once I learn a lesson, I don't forget it. So maybe we can just call a truce, okay? I can live with that. If you're expecting more..."

She didn't finish the sentence, but she didn't really need to, did she?

Cooper took a step back, out of the circle of lamplight. "You should go in. It's getting late."

She didn't like how they were leaving this, but knew there was no other way. "Thank you for the walk home."

She'd turned and taken two steps along her walkway when his voice stopped her once again. "Mel?"

Her heart quaked. Why did this feel like goodbye? Why did it feel final? Final had been three years ago when she'd said she never wanted to speak to him again.

The words had been extreme, but that had been an extreme period in her life.

"I lost two best friends, you know. You might think I sided with Scott, but I didn't. I hated what he was up to and begged him to do the right thing. It was the end of our friendship. I did not condone or support his behavior in any way. You need to know that."

Sadness swept over her. "You didn't stop it," she whispered. "To me, you condoned it by doing nothing."

Silence spun between them, until finally Cooper gave a curt nod and turned, walking away. She watched until the sound of his boots faded and his tall form turned the corner, out of her line of vision.

Only then did she realize that she was still wearing his jacket. She curled her fingers around the edges and pulled it close, drawing in the scents of hay and fresh air and the cologne he'd worn for as long as she could remember. The smell of it was imprinted on her brain, bringing a wealth of memories and emotions. It took her back more years than she cared to count.

She'd worked so hard to put the past behind her, but as the scent of him wrapped around her, she grieved just a little bit for the life she'd nearly had and the dreams she'd lost.

CHAPTER THREE

COOPER SAT IN HIS TRUCK a half block from her flower shop, trying to muster the courage to go in. The other night he had come *this* close to telling her the truth. It had all been going so well. Not quite like old times, but at least they'd been talking. He'd gotten the impression that she'd be open to his apology, so he'd made it.

Only it hadn't gone quite according to plan. She'd pushed. He'd thought for a long time that she hadn't spoken to him for years because of simple pride. The longer the impasse, the harder it was to swallow pride and end it, right? It was difficult to take the first step. But he'd miscalculated. It wasn't just pride with Melissa. He had truly, honestly hurt her.

He'd never intended for things to get so intense the other night. With any other woman he could try flowers to ease his way back into her good graces. Considering Melissa owned the flower shop, he'd had to come up with something else. Besides, she'd see right through that sort of thing.

So a plastic container of his mother's peanut butter chocolate chip cookies sat on the seat beside him as a peace offering. She'd always had a weak spot for those.

He was still trying to figure out what he hoped to achieve by mending fences. Was it simply a need to put the transgressions of his past behind him? To receive absolution from his guilt for the part he'd played in the breakup of her marriage?

Then there was the problem of his feelings for Melissa. They'd been good friends since junior high school. By the time he'd figured out he wanted more, she'd only had eyes for Scott. What was worse, Scott had known how Coop felt, but had never said anything to him. It had been an unspoken rule—that they didn't talk about it. To Scott's credit, he had never rubbed Coop's nose in it. Not until Coop backed him into a corner. Then Scott had shown what sort of man he truly was. And what sort of man Cooper was, too. The kind of guy who would choose to save his own skin rather than do the right thing.

So what did he really want? Coop drummed his fingers on the steering wheel. He considered the idea that maybe he should let her go. Until he did, he couldn't move on. And he really should at some point.

He was twenty-seven years old and he'd never had a serious relationship. All because of Melissa Stone. It went beyond his mom and dad asking when he was going to settle down and give them grandbabies. He wanted that, too. He loved his business, but he wanted a wife and a few kids running around his big empty house. He wanted to teach them to ride and coach their hockey team. More than that, he wanted a partner to share things with. A meal at the end of the day. A beer while watching the football game. A woman he loved waking up beside him in the morning.

It was just that it seemed impossible to make the connection from his life as it was right now to his vision of the future. Melissa—and their unfinished business—was in his way.

So he'd go in there and give her the cookies and get his jacket back and wish her well, and finally, *finally,* move on.

Resolutely, he shut the door to his truck and gripped the dish in sweaty hands. This was stupid, wasn't it? A grown man going home and asking his mother to bake special cookies, of all things. She'd even remembered Melissa's fondness for them. His pulse beat at his wrist and the muscles in his chest tightened with nervousness as he reached for the door. Dammit, he felt about fifteen years old and not anything like a man preparing to let someone go.

Amy Wilkins stood behind the counter, a cordless phone pressed to her ear when he walked in. She looked up and smiled, and his pulse jumped again—not because he was particularly fond of Amy but because she was a notorious flirt and gossip. The last thing he needed was her overhearing anything he'd come to say.

"Cooper?"

He turned to his right and there stood Mel, dressed in a soft sweater the color of red wine and a pair of gray trousers. The sweater draped over her body like some sort of shawl, and it was utterly feminine and flattering. She held a finished bouquet in her hands, an arrangement of red roses, white carnations and baby's breath. Her brown hair was caught up in some sort of clip that left little pieces sticking out. It was one of those casual, purposefully messy looks, and it suited her perfectly.

"Hi," he said, so struck by the sight of her that he lost the few words he'd put together in his mind. Instinctively, he reached for his hat, then remembered he'd left it in the truck.

"Something I can do for you?"

"Um…"

She smiled, but he saw lines of tension around her mouth as her gaze strayed to the front counter. "Let me put this in the cooler."

Amy hung up the phone and tore a piece of paper off a pad. "An order for a get-well arrangement, any color, no more than fifty," she said. "For between five and six."

"I can do that." Melissa pushed open the sliding door to the cooler and put the roses inside. "The Carson arrangement is ready. Joe said he'd be in around three for it."

Cooper shifted his feet as Amy's gaze slid to him. "Something we can do for you, Coop?"

"I, uh…"

He felt Melissa's eyes on him and wondered if he was blushing, because his cheeks suddenly felt on fire. "Sure. I'll take…" Panicking, he scanned the fridge. "Sunflowers. One of those silver buckets with the sunflowers in it."

"Sure thing."

Amy moved to take it out of the cooler, but Melissa's voice stopped her. "I'll get it, Amy. You're already late for your lunch break."

"Oh, I can eat here, I've brought a sand—"

"You wouldn't pick me up a coffee from the Wagon Wheel, would you? I'm not sure I'm going to make it through the afternoon without an extra shot of caffeine."

Amy's gaze slid between Melissa and Cooper. "Oh, sure. Just let me get my purse." She retrieved her bag from beneath the counter. "See you in a bit."

The bell jingled behind her.

"That was probably stupid. It'll be all over the diner, within five minutes of her arrival, that you're in here."

Coop grinned. Amy wasn't a bad sort. She tended to be unlucky in love and a bit vocal about it, but she wasn't intentionally mean or vindictive. "Well, it's probably better than having her eavesdrop."

"Is there something to eavesdrop about?"

He held out the plastic container. "It's a peace offering. For upsetting you the other night."

She came forward and took it from his hands. "Is this what I think it is?" She peeled back the cover and he watched, fascinated, as she closed her eyes and took a deep sniff. "Peanut butter. These are your mom's cookies, aren't they?"

"I remembered they were always your favorites, and begged her to make a batch." He grinned. "You only got half. Sorry."

"I should have had Amy bring me milk instead of coffee." Melissa smiled at him in a genuine, easy way. "Thank you, Cooper."

The warm smile hit him right in the solar plexus, robbing him of breath. "You're welcome. I was thinking about what you said and...I can't change anything that happened. I just want to offer a truce, like you suggested."

"Bygones be bygones, that sort of thing?"

He nodded. "I know you were affected so much more than me, Mel. I'm not disputing that. But the whole thing has hung over me like a black cloud. I know I can't make things right, but will you please accept that I wish I could?"

She put the lid back on the cookies. "Oh Coop," she sighed. "If it were only that easy."

The door jingled and they were interrupted by Callum Shepard. Cooper stood back as the local farmer stepped up to the counter, a wide smile stretched across his face. Cooper was pretty sure he had never seen the normally reticent Callum look quite so happy.

"What can I do for you today, Callum?" Melissa tucked the dish discreetly beneath the counter. "You look like you're in a good mood. Anything to do with the cupcake joint opening up down the street?"

For Pete's sake, the man was practically bouncing in his boots, Cooper thought irritably.

"You heard about that?" Callum asked. "Avery Spencer's opening it. She and Nell are moving here for good."

The latest bombshell in town was finding out that newcomer and all around keep-to-himself kind of guy Callum Shepard had a baby daughter no one knew about.

"That's great," Melissa replied.

"We're getting married," he blurted out, and Cooper nearly choked on a laugh. The guy sounded both thrilled and scared to death.

"Congratulations," Melissa said, smiling. "Have you already done the asking? Or is this wishful thinking?"

Callum finally seemed to chill out and he chuckled. "Sorry. It's still so new. I asked her yesterday and she said yes. But it wasn't planned, so today I'm surprising her with a ring. I thought flowers might be nice to go with it...."

"Absolutely."

Callum seemed to just realize that Cooper was standing there. "Oh, gee. Sorry. You were here first, Cooper."

Coop grinned and held out his hand. "I'm in no rush. Congrats, man."

"Thanks." Callum gripped Cooper's hand and he gave a shake of his head. "You just never know. A year ago the last thing I planned on was getting married and having a kid. Funny how things work out."

"Isn't it?"

Mel interrupted. "What were you thinking, Callum? Something simple, or a grand gesture sort of thing?"

He grinned. "Grand gesture. Roses?"

"Perfect," she decreed. "A dozen, long-stemmed? Maybe in red and white. You can tell her it stands for love and unity."

"That'd be wonderful. Thanks, Melissa."

"It won't take but a minute."

Cooper watched as she deftly selected half a dozen of each color from buckets of roses in the cooler, then arranged them on a huge sheet of green-and-gold floral paper. In no time flat she'd added a touch of greenery and sprig or two of baby's breath and had the bouquet wrapped up and taped and ready to go.

Cooper studied her as she worked. Melissa was good at what she did, and she truly loved the business she'd built. No matter how her life had derailed, she'd landed on her feet and with a smile. She was a strong woman, no doubt about it.

The register dinged as the cash drawer opened and she shut it again, then handed Callum the arrangement and receipt.

"There you go," she said cheerfully. "Good luck."

Cooper wished Callum would hurry up. Before long Amy would be back and any chance to finish his conversation with Mel privately would be gone. But the farmer had other ideas.

"One more thing…I picked out this ring today, but I'm not sure she'll like it. Would you mind…?"

Callum reached into his pocket and pulled out a box. He handed it across the counter and Melissa flipped open the lid. It creaked, as all jewelry boxes did, and she looked down at what nestled inside.

Cooper couldn't see what the ring looked like, but he could see the way Melissa's face softened as she gazed upon it with a mix of wistfulness and tenderness, pain and happiness.

"It's beautiful, Callum. Just gorgeous."

She closed the box and handed it back. "Avery's a lucky woman. I know you'll be very happy together."

"Thanks," he replied. "And thanks for the flowers."

"You're welcome."

"Go get 'em, tiger," Coop said, lifting a hand as Callum made for the exit.

"He's excited," Melissa observed as the door clicked shut.

"He's marrying the woman he loves. Of course he's excited." Cooper surprised himself with his sentimental observation. Seeing Melissa look at that engagement ring had affected him more than he cared to admit. She deserved something like that. Happiness. She certainly deserved better than what she'd gotten the first time around.

"Well, I hope it all works out for them," she replied, tidying up her countertop.

"Why shouldn't it? Just because your marriage didn't work doesn't mean every couple is doomed to unhappiness."

"I know that." She looked hurt at his observation.

He stepped closer to the counter. "I didn't mean that the way it sounded. I just meant... you can't stop believing in love just because it didn't work out once before."

"Did I say I had stopped believing?" Her hands paused on the tape dispenser.

"No."

She fussed about, but he could tell she was just trying to keep busy.

"So, have you considered giving it another try?" he asked.

"No."

"Why not?"

She looked up at him sharply. "Just because

it exists doesn't mean it exists for *me,* okay? Why the sudden interest? Boy, you've been all up in my business lately. Thanks for the cookies, Coop, and we can shake hands and let bygones be bygones like you wanted. But let's just leave it at that, okay?"

He looked out the display window and saw Amy turning the corner, coming down the block. He frowned. "You mean that? About letting bygones be bygones?"

"Sure."

"Then shake on it, like you said."

He held out his hand and waited. Silently counted the seconds. Amy would be back at any moment, curse her busybody self.

Slowly Mel's hand stretched out. Met his. Her fingers curled around his palm.

Her skin was warm, her fingers slightly callused from working with flowers and chemicals all day long. He turned her hand over in his, looked at the close-clipped, unpolished fingernails that were part of the profession she'd chosen. Years ago she'd grown them long and always had them painted.

Mel wasn't the same girl he remembered, and perhaps it was time he accepted that.

She slid her fingers from his while a strange

silence filled the shop. "There," she finally said, her voice oddly tight. "Truce."

"Truce."

The word seemed hollow somehow, and left him wanting more. So much more it left him floundering.

"Mel…"

Amy came back inside, rosy-cheeked and bringing a rush of fall wind with her. "One coffee, cream and sugar, just as ordered," she announced brightly.

It was time Cooper got out of there. He'd done what he'd set out to do—given her the cookies and made peace between them. More than that, he'd realized that all this time he'd been holding on to a vision of the girl he'd once known and loved, rather than the woman she'd become.

"I'll see you around, Mel," he said quietly. "Amy."

"See you around," Melissa replied, while her assistant merely smiled and gave a waggle of her fingers.

Outside the shop the air had turned suddenly cold. Coop shivered as he realized two very annoying things.

First of all, he'd forgotten to ask for his jacket back.

And second, his whole plan had backfired. Instead of letting go so he could move forward, he was starting to realize that the woman Melissa had become could be even more of a threat to his heart than the girl she'd once been.

Melissa watched Coop walk down the street, and tried hard to ignore the shocking way her stomach seemed to be tangling in knots. Her pulse still raced, beating at the hollow of her wrist where his fingers had rested only moments ago. That had been no ordinary handshake. Things had *tingled.* In a way they hadn't since she'd been sixteen and had finally given up on him ever looking at her as if she was a girl. Scott had kissed her one night after a school dance and that had been the end of any crushes on Coop. She'd accepted that they'd only just be friends. It had been fine while she'd dated Scott, and after, when she'd married him. Coop had ended up being more like a brother.

And when the divorce happened, there certainly hadn't been any romantic feelings. She'd despised him too much for any tingling or shortness of breath.

So why was she feeling it today, after all these years?

"You okay, Melissa?" Amy's voice cut through the clutter of her thoughts and drew her eyes from Cooper, who was now getting into the cab of his truck.

"Oh, sure! Thanks for bringing the coffee."

"Cooper never took his flowers," Amy commented, her perfectly plucked brows crinkling. "Should I go after him?"

Mel shook her head quickly. "Oh, he changed his mind." She reached under the counter and brought out the plastic dish. "Want a cookie?"

"Cooper Ford brought you cookies?"

She shrugged. "I know you're a few years younger than we are, but Coop and a bunch of us were friends in school. We all used to hang out." She scrambled to cover, to make it no big deal, because she knew Amy would definitely make something out of it. "Ask anyone in our group and they'd remember Jean Ford's peanut butter chocolate chip cookies."

Amy reached into the container and took one. "Coop's kind of funny. He used to date a lot, but the last few years I've hardly seen him with anyone." She scowled. "I asked him out once, you know. He turned me down. Said I was too young for him. Shoot, he was twenty-five and I was twenty-two. Not that much of a difference."

Melissa felt as if she were walking in a field of land mines. Amy's disastrous love life was nearly a thing of legend in Cadence Creek. It was a shame, really, because Amy was a nice girl. She had a generous heart and would do anything for someone in need. For a while it looked as though she and Sam Diamond would become an item, but that had gone south. In Mel's opinion, if Amy had one fault, it was that she had difficulty hiding her feelings—and she did tend to get hurt quite easily. When she did, everyone in the county ended up hearing about it.

"Well," Melissa said carefully, "if he hasn't been dating, then you know it wasn't just about you."

But the news that Coop hadn't been dating made her curious. Why not? Had someone broken his heart? She'd been so wrapped up in her own relationship failure, she knew nothing about his love life.

Not that it mattered. It was no less than he deserved, after years of playing the field with such enthusiasm. Perhaps everyone else had clued in to the kind of man he was, the way she had.

That's not fair, a voice inside her head protested. Melissa tried to quiet that voice, but it persisted. *Cooper Ford is a good man. A good man who made a bad choice.*

"Huh." She gave a huff of disbelief that sounded overly loud in the little shop.

"What?" Amy asked, nibbling on a cookie.

"Oh." Melissa's cheeks heated and she hid behind her coffee cup, taking a sip that nearly scalded the inside of her mouth. She swallowed painfully and blinked. "Nothing, really. I was just thinking about something." Like how she suddenly seemed to be forgetting all the reasons she had for disliking Cooper. He'd basically condoned Scott's affair by doing nothing. That was a pretty good indication of his view of how to treat a woman.

Amy grinned. "Yeah, thinking about Cooper Ford, I bet. Just because he turned me down doesn't mean I don't have eyes in my head. I bet you could bounce quarters off that butt."

Melissa figured Amy was right. There was absolutely nothing wrong with Cooper's looks. That had never been an issue.

She dropped what was left of her cookie in the trash can and brushed her hands. "Maybe, but you don't have a relationship with a guy's butt, Amy. It's about a lot more than that. Believe me, I wouldn't go near Cooper Ford in *that* way with a ten-foot pole."

She moved off to the workroom to get started on the get-well arrangement, but could still feel Amy's gaze on her as she moved around, gathering materials.

It was a good thing Amy hadn't seen Mel and

Cooper on Saturday night, then. Because she'd come very close to going after Cooper Ford in exactly that way. Looking at the stars while swinging in the park? Come on.

It had been a momentary lapse, and that was all. Because Mel was smarter now. She had no plans to enter any relationship, but if she did?

It would sure as shootin' be with someone more trustworthy than Coop.

CHAPTER FOUR

MEL SIGNED UP to volunteer at the construction site a few more times. Stu and his family would be able to move in within a week or so, and now it was down to the finishing touches. Bifold doors were being hung for the bedroom closets. The appliances arrived, and on a particularly warm afternoon in late September, the washer and dryer were installed while heavy equipment worked outside, leveling what would be the front yard. It was too late to seed or sod, but come next spring, the ground would be ready.

By choosing afternoon time slots, Melissa had figured she'd miss seeing Coop. He tended to quit by lunchtime so he could get back and look after things at the Double C. It was just easier if they kept their distance from each other. The last thing she needed was to be getting ideas. A truce was one thing, but she wasn't stupid. She knew what that tingly, breathless sensation meant, and it would only mean trouble—for both of them.

In another week she should know for sure if the last attempt at the clinic had been a success. Until then, she was simply keeping herself busy to make the time go faster. She made sure she was eating right, just in case, and that she got a good seven to eight hours' sleep every night. If by some miracle she'd conceived, she was determined to do everything right from the start. She'd even cut back on her caffeine consumption, drinking only half-caf in the mornings.

She was just taking a pot of bronze mums out of the trunk of her car when she saw the familiar brown half-ton pull into the yard.

She inhaled and exhaled deeply. Okay. Just because Coop and she were both here didn't mean they had to work on the same thing. She'd done a good job of avoiding him for years. She could manage to be in the same general area and not speak a word to him. She'd done it tons of times in the past.

Except there was one problem. Coop had always made a point of avoiding her, too, and now he wasn't. It was way harder to ignore someone who didn't ignore you in return.

"Hey, Mel."

His voice came from behind her, warm and smooth. She tried very hard not to sigh. Instead, she picked up the huge pot and turned around, half hiding behind the greenery and rusty-orange blossoms.

"Cooper. Excuse me, please."

He reached out. "Let me take that for you."

"It's fine. I've got it."

She started off toward the porch. The mums would look great flanking the front steps, out of the way of the wheelchair ramp that had been built in anticipation of Cheryl's declining health. Mel put the pot down and spun it so the blooms showed to best advantage. When she turned to go back to her car for the second pot, she nearly ran smack into Coop, who was right behind her, carrying the partner arrangement.

"Thought I'd bring the other one."

She gritted her teeth. "Fine. Put it on the other side." She darted away to grab her supplies and shut her trunk.

He'd put the pot in the precise spot she'd wanted, and was waiting as she approached the steps. "What else have you got?" he asked pleasantly.

She wrinkled her brow. "Don't you have something to hammer or nail or screw or something?"

He burst out laughing. She blushed. She could feel it flood her cheeks and neck, and her tone grew even more irritated. "Oh, you know what I mean! What are you, twelve?"

It only made him laugh harder. "What is so damned funny?" she demanded.

"You!" He paused and wiped his eyes. "Some truce," he commented. "You're meaner than ever."

"Having a truce does not make us besties all of a sudden," she said acidly, moving past him and up the steps.

"Clearly," he answered, following her.

She had more going on in her life than he could imagine, certainly more than worrying about what he thought of her. She tried to envision his face if she told him she was possibly pregnant by a sperm donor. He'd swallow his tongue. She nearly did tell him, just for the shock value.

But she kept silent, knowing this was too important to joke about. She frowned. A lot of people in this town would talk behind their hands if they knew what she'd been planning. She'd thought about that a lot while making her decision. She had a business here. Family. It was a very small town. Not everyone was that forward thinking. They still thought the correct order of things was to meet someone, get married and then start a family.

Truth was, she tended to agree with that assessment in most cases. But real life wasn't always that neat and tidy, and in her world, a girl had to do what she had to do. Melissa was responsible for her own happiness, and damn public opinion.

She reached into her canvas bag and pulled out a wooden pole and bracket, a small cordless drill and a flat packet that contained a rectangle of brightly colored nylon. She liked the homey touch of a decorative flag. This one was in autumn hues, a collage of fall leaves in yellows, oranges, reds and browns, with the word Welcome across the bottom.

"What's that?"

She took the pole and bracket out of the plastic sheathing. "It's a flag. I'll mount the bracket here, on the porch pillar, and then put the flag up."

"Need a hand with that?"

"Not really." She took out the screws, set the bracket against the post and held it there with her forearm while she placed a screw on the drill bit. It wobbled and she shifted, which made the bracket slip so that it was off center.

"Pride goes before the fall," Coop noted.

She refused to look at him. "I'm hardly in danger of falling."

He chuckled. "The saying isn't literal, you know. Here, let me hold the bracket while you set the screw."

She could refuse, but if the stupid thing slipped again she was going to look like an idiot. And she did appreciate the fact that he was offering to help rather than do it for her, the way most men would. "Fine. Just make sure it's centered."

He held it and she put in the first screw, then the second.

"Thanks," she said quietly. "It won't move now. I can put the last ones in just fine."

He didn't leave as she finished fastening the bracket. Instead he opened the package and unfolded the flag. "This is nice," he said, spreading out the nylon.

"I know Cheryl tires so easily with her MS. She's going to want to pick stuff out herself, but a few touches here and there might make this seem homey right away."

Melissa took the flag from his hand and threaded the pole through the pocket. Then she slid the stick into the bracket, tightened the screw to hold it in place, and it was done. The flag rippled gently in the warm westerly breeze. *Welcome.*

"There," she said, standing back and putting

her hands on her hips. "I should see what else there is to do."

She left Coop standing on the porch while she went inside to find the coordinator and get her assignment.

It turned out that the big project of the day was constructing the deck, so Melissa made her way to the back of the house. Six-by-six posts were stuck in concrete blocks, and a group of men, Cooper included, were finishing the construction of all the support pieces. A pile of decking sat to one side, waiting to be cut into the appropriate lengths and screwed down. A makeshift table of sawhorses and plywood held a box of coffee from the shop out on the highway, as well as two brown boxes half depleted of doughnuts.

When Cooper saw her standing to the side, he tilted back his hat. "Hey, George," he called out. "Melissa there is pretty handy with a drill. You should get her set up with a belt and a pouch of screws."

George Grant, a retired farmer, pushed back his own cap. "That true, Miss Stone?"

She lifted her arm as if she were holding a pistol. "I brought my own." And she knew how to use it. Maybe she wasn't up to speed on brad nailers and miter saws and everything else, but she did most of the upkeep on her property herself. Having a drill, a set of screwdrivers and pliers had come in very handy over the years.

George laughed, a good-natured wheeze. "Of course you did. Well, give us a few minutes and we'll be ready to put you to work. Gonna start cutting the decking real soon."

Cooper threw her a wink that she ignored. Just as she ignored his dusty boots, snug jeans and the way his chest filled out a plaid shirt and fleece vest. The Double C brand decorated the left breast, one *C* nestled within the other.

She understood that he was sorry for what had happened. She was even willing to call a truce. But there was a long way to go to reestablish trust, or even respect. She could forgive him for making a bad judgment call. That didn't mean she was naive enough to let him close enough to have an impact on her life again. Throw her own surprising reaction into the midst and she'd prefer to stay as far away from Coop as possible.

There were enough people around that she was spared having to engage in much conversation. Instead she worked steadily, lining up the decking and screwing it down to the supports. It wasn't an overly large deck, but the Dickinsons would be able to put a barbecue on it, along with a set of patio furniture for enjoying warm summer days. Since it was south facing, it would get a lot of sun, and as the structure took shape Mel could envision pots of flowers and herbs blooming there. The afternoon waned, the floor of the deck was done, and as a group they began working on the railing. It was past five, then past six, but everyone silently agreed that they'd come this close to finishing and may as well carry on.

At quarter to seven they were finally done, and spent another ten minutes picking up wood scraps and storing everything in the garage. As Mel walked to her car, Cooper fell in step beside her. "That was good work today," he said. "Long, but good."

"It's all pretty much done now, isn't it?" she asked, reaching her car door and opening it. She threw her purse inside and then bent to carefully place the drill on the seat.

"The official unveiling is next Saturday. Are you coming?"

"Oh." She straightened, resting one arm on the top of the open door. "I hadn't actually heard about it."

"We're doing a spit roast. Side of beef, half a pig, baked beans, you know the drill. Make it a real housewarming for them."

"That's nice."

He gave a small shrug. "Like I said, Stu's one

of my guys. I'm happy to help. Mom's organizing the food stuff, but I think we're just asking people who are coming to bring some sort of dessert. You should try to make it."

"We'll see." It did sound like fun, and it was going to be a community event so they wouldn't be in each other's face the whole time. It wasn't like this was a date or anything.

"I'd better go. I was gone a long time today," Coop said. "I need to check on things at the barns and grab some dinner. I'll see you around, Mel."

He walked away. She watched the movement of his shoulders as he reached into his pocket for his keys, and then admired the length of his legs as he put one foot in his truck and swung himself up into the seat. Amy had commented that he hadn't dated much in the last few years. Again Melissa wondered why, because during the years she and Scott had been married, he'd gone through a bunch of girlfriends, none of them lasting more than a few months. Cooper had broken his share of hearts.

Dust flew up from his tires as he backed up, turned around and headed out the driveway toward the road.

She'd thought he played the field a little too enthusiastically, but she realized now that Amy was right. The last few years Melissa hadn't seen him with anyone on his arm. He'd said that he'd been really angry with Scott about the affair. Had that event made Coop take a look in the mirror?

Maybe she really hadn't been the only one affected by the situation. After all, Scott had left town. She hadn't realized that Coop's friendship with him had ended so completely, as well. She'd kind of figured they'd stayed in touch.

She got behind the wheel of her car and sighed. Tonight he hadn't made the slightest suggestion that they go for coffee or a bite to eat. Not that she'd wanted him to, but their last few encounters he'd been pressing his case.

Apparently he'd finally gotten the message. There was no earthly reason why she should be feeling let down about that, but she was. As she turned in the opposite direction from Coop, she laughed a little. Maybe all this indecision was just hormones.

A girl could hope, after all.

Mel went right from the shop to the housewarming, carrying her favorite caramel bread pudding in a covered glass dish. She'd dressed for the weather, which had turned quite cool at the end of September. There was a frost warning for tonight, and even though there were rumors of a bonfire happening later, she knew it would get chilly. She wore skinny jeans and her favorite black boots that came to just below the knee, a raspberry-colored tailored shirt and a multicolored scarf twisted around her neck. Over that she had on a charcoal sweater-coat.

Cars lined the lane when she arrived, and she had to park nearly out at the road and walk in. Country music came from a stereo somewhere, getting louder as she approached the house. From a hundred yards she could make out the sign draped over the eaves of the front porch: Welcome Home.

Melissa smiled and felt a lump rise in her throat. It was a good thing they'd done here, and so typical of Cadence Creek. Despite the lack of privacy, and the fact that everyone was aware of her history, she knew she didn't want to live anywhere else. It was home. She just hoped they'd be as welcoming to her if and when she showed up expecting a baby.

She should know anytime. Her period had been due a few days ago and she'd done a home pregnancy test right away. It had been negative, but she wasn't giving up hope. The fact that she hadn't started yet was a good sign. False negatives happened.

But for tonight she was not going to think about it. Instead she was going to focus on enjoying herself.

She went straight to the open garage and put her dessert on a table along with the rest—a staggering array of cakes, pies and pans of unnamed things that generally started out with a graham-cracker crust and ended with whipped cream on top. There was a carousel of gorgeous-looking cupcakes, too, which had probably come from Callum and Avery.

Mel said hello to the Diamond family couples—Sam and Angela, and Tyson and Clara—before moving on to their hired hand, Rhys Bullock, and then Callum and Avery. Amy had come with a date that Melissa didn't recognize, and she gave a wave across the yard. Finally she reached Stu and Cheryl, both of whom were beaming.

Mel reached up and hugged Stu. "Happy housewarming."

He squeezed her back. "Thanks. This community…" He just shook his head, overcome with emotion.

"I know," she replied. "And Stu, don't think we all don't realize that you'd do the same for any of us." She turned her attention to Cheryl. In her early forties, his wife was an attractive woman with a few gray strands in her hair and a little extra weight around her middle from bearing her children. She had a rough time of it with her MS, but tonight her wheelchair was tucked away and she was making do with just a cane as she enjoyed the party.

"Cheryl," Melissa said warmly, reaching out and squeezing her arm. "How do you like your new house?"

Cheryl smiled. "It's beautiful. The kids already have their rooms picked out. And everything on the main floor makes it so much easier for me." She leaned against Stu, who put his arm around her. "We've got furniture coming on Monday. I haven't been this excited since we got married and moved into our first apartment."

Mel's heart gave a little pang as she watched the two of them. The couple personified wedding vows, in particular the loving and cherishing part, and in the sickness and in health. She hoped they knew how lucky they were. In one way it was reassuring to know that sort of love truly did exist. In another it was a letdown to know that at one time she'd made those promises and meant them, and it still hadn't been enough.

Stu gave a nod at something behind her and she turned around. Cooper was standing before a huge metal grill, laughing at something Rhys was saying.

"I don't know how I'll ever repay Coop, though," Stu mused. "He's a good boss. And a better friend. I know how much he had to do with this project, and I know he's responsible for tonight."

Melissa's eyes were drawn to the sight of Coop laughing as he shut the lid on the grill. As if he'd known she was watching, his gaze lifted and met hers, and he gave an almost imperceptible nod and touched the brim of his hat.

It was utterly unfair that her heart pattered.

"Excuse me," she murmured, moving away and out of Coop's line of vision. "I think I'm going to get a drink."

She meandered over to the folding tables set up with paper plates, cutlery and cups, and coolers underneath. Instead of taking a cup, she popped the top on a can of soda and took a drink.

"Melissa, dear, how are you?"

She spun to find Molly Diamond behind her, wearing a broad grin.

"Molly. I'm fine, how are you?" She went forward and gave the older woman a hug.

"Oh, I'm right as rain. Got a couple of grandbabies and another on the way, and Callum and

Avery are around a lot with Nell. They keep me busy. Keep me young."

"At least you have grandkids," another voice grumbled.

Melissa laughed and turned. "Oh my goodness. Hello, Mrs. Ford." Cooper's mother. Mel had spent hours in her kitchen when she and her gang had been kids, hanging out after school or getting together for movies on a Friday night. They'd been partial to horror flicks, Mel recalled, and Jean had always provided popcorn and potato chips.

"Call me Jean, like you used to," Coop's mother ordered. "Haven't seen you around much, Melissa. You keeping busy?"

She nodded. "The store takes up most of my time."

"The flowers Cooper bought for my birthday were lovely. How'd you like the cookies?"

"Cookies?" Molly asked.

"Cooper got me to whip up a special batch," Jean confided. "Peanut butter chocolate chip. He hasn't asked for those in years, and I remembered they were Melissa's favorites." She looked at her with a twinkle in her eye. "Did you share?"

Melissa didn't quite know what to say. It would probably be best to make a joke out of it, dispel any matchmaking inklings Molly and Jean might come up with if they put their heads together. Mel and Coop were both single, and in a town this size, pairing people up was a popular pastime. "Of course I didn't share. I made Coop eat crow pie."

Molly and Jean laughed. "Good girl. Coop needs someone to keep him on his toes."

"Oh, it's definitely not like that."

"Too bad," Jean observed. "I always liked having you around." She put a hand on Mel's shoulder. "I know you and Coop had a blowup when you and Scott split. I hope you've worked it out now. You were always such good friends. He needs that."

So Jean didn't know what had caused their rift? Interesting.

"The past is in the past," Mel said, trying to sound breezy. "Sometimes you have to stand on your own two feet and get on with it, you know?"

"Atta girl," Molly praised.

"I just wish Coop would get on with settling down. I could use a grandbaby or two of my own to spoil."

Someone started clanging a triangle, calling everyone to dinner, which was convenient, since Mel's palm had absently strayed to her flat tummy at Jean's words. She'd never been mad at Jean, and in fact she'd missed Coop's parents almost as much as she'd missed him.

If she was pregnant, it might be nice to have someone like Jean to give her baby cuddles. She rather hoped her own parents would fill that role, but last spring she'd let them in on her plans and they'd expressed dismay rather than support. Like most people, they thought she should just wait, maybe see if she was going to get married again.

Things had been tense in their relationship ever since. Normally they'd be front and center at an event like this, but since taking early retirement a few months before, the Stones were on a long-overdue vacation. New England in the fall. There'd only been one email since their departure, letting Melissa know they'd arrived safely. No updates or pictures sent. She didn't much like being out of favor with them, but she had a right to make her own decisions.

For the next half hour, the throng settled in lawn chairs and on steps to eat the tender beef, succulent roast pork, baked beans, fresh rolls and coleslaw. It got dark, and patio lanterns were turned on and the bonfire lit. When the main meal was over, everyone wandered into the garage for dessert and a cup of coffee that was brewing in the big urns borrowed from the church. Mel left the coffee alone, but wasn't so disciplined when it came to dessert. She helped herself to a small piece of carrot cake with cream cheese frosting, a sliver of apple pie and a piece of something that could only be described as a mound of dark chocolate sin. There were at least a dozen other gorgeous-looking desserts, but she had only so much room.

She found a quiet corner where she could stand back and watch. Now that the fire had burned awhile, she saw Coop and Sam Diamond set up the kids with sticks and marshmallows for roasting. The stereo was turned off when someone got out a guitar and started taking requests. She sighed, letting the day's fatigue and her full belly lull her into a mellow state of mind. She loved Cadence Creek. Always had. She'd never lived anywhere else nor did she want to. Maybe that was why the acceptance was so important.

When her marriage had hit the skids, there'd been a lot of long faces and sympathy to go around. On one level it had driven her bonkers—both the continual "so sorry" sentiments and the knowledge that she was gossip fodder. But on another, it had felt good knowing people cared. And they'd certainly supported her business when she'd opened her doors short months later.

A cramp slid across her belly. Boy, she'd overdone it with the cake, hadn't she? That and beans and so much meat were bound to give her some indigestion. She frowned. Except it didn't feel like indigestion. It felt heavy and…

She swallowed. She knew that feeling. Not now. Not here. Dammit, not again.

With a wooden smile, she made her way through the garage and into the house. She knew exactly where the half bath was, and made a beeline for it, clutching her purse handle with tight fingers.

And when she saw that she'd been right—not indigestion at all—she fought to keep from crying. She'd wanted this time to be the one, so very badly. She'd been so *sure*. But wanting something desperately did not make it so, and for a second she bit down on her lip as two hot tears slid out of the corners of her eyes.

She brushed them away immediately. She had to go back out there. People were going to see her. She did not want them to notice red eyes and blotchy cheeks and a wobbly lip. A wobbly lip that quivered despite her best attempts to stop it…

She gasped, bracing her hands on the edge of

the sink, trying to catch her breath as the truth settled, hard and uncompromising. She'd let herself hope again. She'd done everything right— paid the money, had the procedure, watched what she ate and drank and how much she slept, how much she lifted at the store, and still...

Words scrolled across her brain like a profane ticker tape of frustration.

At the same time, her heart was breaking. She only wanted this one thing. Hadn't she earned it? She'd been hurt and humiliated and abandoned, and she'd picked herself up, brushed herself off, and got on with it. She'd planned everything so carefully, so why wasn't it working?

Melissa jumped as a knock sounded on the door. "Anyone in there?"

She inhaled and straightened. "Be right out!" she called with false brightness, then turned on the water in the sink.

She dried her hands, pressed them to her face and willed herself to hold it together.

Clara Diamond was on the other side of the door—pregnant, beautiful Clara Diamond with glowing, rosy cheeks. "Oh, hi, Melissa," she chirped. "Sorry to rush you. My bladder seems to hold only a teaspoon right now."

The words stabbed into her. She smiled. "It's all yours," she said, making her way to the garage door, down the aisle between the tables and straight out the driveway to the parked cars. She loved Clara, she really did, but seeing her at that precise moment was salt in the wound, and it stung.

Mel held it all in, every last bit of emotion, until she was past the crowd and flanked only by the shadows of parked vehicles. As soon as she was certain no one would hear her, she tried gulping in some air. The air went in just fine, but shocked her when it came out on a sob. She frantically tried to reel it back in, but it was too late. First there was one, then another, and the next thing she knew she was stumbling her way to her car, hiccuping and half crying.

"Mel!"

Oh crap. She knew that voice. It was the voice of a man who suddenly couldn't seem to let well enough alone, and he was the last person she wanted to talk to right now. She shoved her hand into her purse, desperately searching for keys. She could get inside her car and lock the door. He wouldn't see her face then. She hooked her finger on the key ring. She could hear his boots on the dirt and he called her name again. "Mel! What's going on?"

She scrambled to hit the button to unlock the doors—and dropped the keys.

She was not going to be able to hold herself together for very long.

There was no light this far from the house and she crouched, frantically feeling for her key ring. It was too late. Cooper reached her and knelt down. "Mel, what's wrong?"

"I dropped my keys." She tried to sound normal, but her voice was thick.

"That's not what's wrong. You were running and crying. What the hell happened?"

A spurt of anger rushed through her. "Oh, what do you care, Cooper Ford?"

"I care," he said simply.

She found the keys and stood up, though her fingers shook. "You don't have a right to care!"

It felt good to be angry. To lash out. She had a sinking feeling that it wasn't really Cooper she was mad at, but it didn't matter. He made a great target.

He gave an impatient sound. "News flash, Melissa. You don't, and have never had, the right to tell me who I can or can't care about! So if I want to care, I'll damn well care, all right?"

She stared at him in stunned silence for a breath.

And then completely embarrassed herself by bursting into tears and throwing herself into his arms.

CHAPTER FIVE

MELISSA CAME BARRELING at his chest, forcing Coop to take a step backward as his arms instinctively came around her.

He hadn't meant to yell at her. He especially hadn't meant to make her cry, or at least cry more than she already had been. His throat tightened. She was in all-out sobbing mode now. Thank goodness they were sheltered from any light from the fire, and far enough away that no one would hear. He knew Mel well enough to know that she would want to keep a meltdown private. What he didn't understand was what had set her off in the first place.

Her sweater was bulky and the crazy scarf she wore tangled with her hair. Cooper pressed his hand to the back of her head and, unsure of what else to say, murmured, "It's okay. Whatever it is, Mel, it'll be fine."

"It won't be fine," she replied, half wailing.

"You don't know, Coop! It hasn't been *fine* for three years now!"

Three years. Ever since Scott left. Cooper had figured that as the months passed he'd be less angry about it. But seeing how it tore Mel apart—after all this time—brought those feelings back again. She had deserved so much better. The fact that she still seemed to carry a torch for the guy made Coop want to hit something.

But he kept a lid on it, forcing gentleness into his voice. "What don't I know?"

"You don't know anything!"

Coop figured the best thing to do now was let her cry and get it out of her system. He'd seen her upset before; they'd known each other for two decades, after all. And he'd seen her angry. Angry at him. Definitely angry at Scott. But even in the anger there'd been an underlying layer of hurt. She'd been betrayed. And she'd loved Scott. Coop knew that without a doubt.

"I don't know anything," he confirmed softly, holding her close, his heart contracting at the sad sounds muffled against his coat. Knowing she was hurting so much only made him feel worse about himself. He'd always been the sort of guy whose creed was that honesty was the best policy even when it meant taking your lumps. He hadn't been honest with her. He'd hidden the truth from his best friend for the very worst of reasons: to protect himself.

He didn't like what that said about the kind of man he'd become. Hadn't Scott done the exact same thing? Lied to cover his own butt? Coop was no better than Scott had been in the end.

"You don't know," she continued. "All our plans. My plans." She hiccuped a sob. "And I've tried so hard to do it all alone, but this one thing…I keep failing and it hurts. Oh, it hurts, Coop."

He just held her tighter.

Finally, he pulled back a little, keeping his hands on her upper arms. "Let me take you home. I don't want you driving like this."

"I'm fine…."

He cursed. "You are not fine. You're not even in the same postal code as fine. You're tired and upset. Give me your keys, Mel."

"What will you do? You can't walk home…."

He was relieved she was capitulating. "I've got my cell. I'll call Mom or Dad. One of them will come get me in the truck."

"And have them know what just happened? No, thank you. I promise I'm fine to drive."

My, she was obstinate. "And I say you're not. Look at you. You're shaking."

She slid the keys into his palm. "You're so stubborn."

He tried to smile. Yeah, weren't they just peas in a pod? "Glad you remember."

He held the door for her and she slid into the passenger seat. As he got behind the wheel, he found his knees pressed against it. He reached for the lever to adjust the seat, mercifully sliding it back into a more comfortable position. Her compact was so much smaller than his truck, but it was economical and suited her purposes, didn't it? He turned the car around and stopped only briefly at the corner where the driveway met the road.

"You want to tell me what's got you so upset?" he asked quietly. "You kind of lost it back there."

"It's nothing."

He looked over. She was staring out the window, her jaw set in a mulish way he recognized. "I think we both know that you crying in my arms is not nothing."

She sighed, a tremulous sound that proved to him she wasn't quite put back together yet.

"If I tell you, you'll either laugh or tell me I'm crazy, and I'd rather save myself the trouble."

He slowed down as they entered the main part of town. "I promise I won't laugh or tell you you're crazy."

When Mel still didn't spill, Coop tightened his grip on the steering wheel. More and more he'd been wondering about her feelings for Scott. He'd hoped she didn't still love him. She needed to get over him and move on, with someone who would treat her right.

His fingers tightened on the steering wheel. Someone like him?

Right. He'd blown that chance twice already.

In a matter of seconds they were pulling up in front of her house. He turned into the driveway and killed the engine. Still Mel said nothing. She simply gathered up her purse and opened her door.

With a put-upon sigh, Coop got out, too. If she wasn't going to say anything, he'd call his dad and get him to bring the truck. He was just reaching into his pocket when the motion light at her front steps came on, illuminating her face.

Her lower lip was still wobbling. Just a little, but he got the feeling that she'd step inside her house, shut the door and start crying again.

He should let her go, and not get in the middle of whatever it was that had her so upset. One minute she'd been fine at the party, and the next…had someone said something to her? And then there was the knowledge that he'd failed her once before when she was in trouble. If she needed help, he couldn't walk away again.

"Mel…" He reached out and took her hand. It was meant to be a gesture of consolation, of comfort. But the moment he felt her soft skin against his, the familiar feelings kicked in.

He knew he shouldn't, but it tore him up to see her so upset. When she lifted her gaze to his, for a split second it felt as if all the oxygen had left his body. Moisture clung to her lower lashes. Her hair curled around her face, so similar to how it used to when they were teenagers and he'd longed to tell her how he felt, only he couldn't, because she was Scott's girl.

He'd waited long enough to find out, hadn't he? Over ten long, torturous years.

Before she could respond, he leaned forward and kissed her.

There was a brief moment of surprise when she froze beneath him and his lips hovered, barely touching hers. And then she moved her mouth, the tiniest little nibble on his lower lip, shyly inviting him in.

His whole body vibrated as he forced himself to go slowly, slowly. He still held her hand, but his right arm went around her waist, pulling her closer until her soft sweater was pressed against his fleece. He angled his head a little and gave a small nudge, urging her to open her mouth wider. Oh God—she tasted like chocolate and spice and woman. So much better than he'd ever dreamed.

"Mel," he whispered, awed. "Mel."

A little of the fragile control he held snapped, and he kissed her again, more urgently this time. Her arms slipped around his neck and she made a little sound in her throat, the soft vibration of it rippling through his entire body. Her front door was just behind them, and he reached for her hips, settling her against the painted steel, pressing his body closer to hers.

He slid his lips off her mouth and tasted the skin where the graceful column of her neck met her ear. Her pelvis rubbed against his and he started to lose his ability to be rational.

Panic threaded its way through Mel's veins. This couldn't be happening. For heaven's sake, she'd given up hoping for anything physical with Coop when she was sixteen. She'd fallen for Scott. There'd never been any…anything between her and Coop after that. She'd outgrown her crush, right?

Clearly not, because he was sliding his tongue down her neck and she loved every second of it. And this could not happen. It could *not*.

"Stop. Coop...please stop."

Slowly he relaxed his body, putting a few inches between them. The column of her neck was cool where the air touched the damp skin. The sound of their heavy breathing was loud in the dark silence. "Oh my God," she whispered. On top of everything else that had scrambled her emotions today, necking with Coop only made matters worse. "We're standing right in the middle of the light. How could you do this?" She turned her head and scanned the neighbors' yards. Had anyone seen?

Her body was still humming from the feel of him pressed against her, and when she challenged him with her eyes, he glared back. With a grunt of frustration, he tugged on her wrist and pulled her away from the door and the circle of light.

"What the hell is going on with you?" he demanded. "First you throw yourself in my arms, then you won't say a thing. Then you wrap your arms around my neck and kiss me, and then accuse me of...what are you accusing me of again? Mel, make up your damned mind!"

She ran an agitated hand through her hair. This was going all wrong. She was supposed to come home, go inside and fall apart. She wasn't supposed to be skulking in dark corners with

Cooper! But his question brought her back to the present with a thud. The truth was, she was a mess. She didn't know what she was feeling. So when he gave her arm a little shake, she snapped her head up and blurted out, "Look, I got my period, okay?"

His hands dropped to his sides. He groaned. "That's a little TMI, isn't it? All of this is because you're hormonal?"

This time she drew back and punched him in the arm. "No, you idiot! I've been trying to have a baby!"

The words rippled through the air and she immediately pressed a hand to her mouth. She hadn't meant to say it. Especially not like *that*.

Coop's face went white and he looked as if he needed to sit down to digest what she'd just said. Stunned, he made his way to the stoop, motion light and all, and dropped his weight on the third step. "You've been...holy hell. With who?"

He turned his face toward her. Heat rose to her cheeks in embarrassment. For years she'd ignored the fact that once upon a time she'd have done anything to have his hands and lips on her like they'd been only moments ago. Now that they had been...it took her back to those days of desperately trying to get his attention. To make him see her as more than just a friend. And now he thought she was sexually involved with some-one. At any other time it would be comical. In light of the situation, it was just plain awkward. "It's none of your business."

He swallowed, then turned those cursed bed-room eyes on her. He looked up at her from be-neath those sooty lashes and said ominously, "From the way you were kissing me a moment ago, I'd say it is very much my business."

"I was not kissing you! I mean, I was, but it was just that I'm such a mess and, oh Coop, you always complicate everything!"

Complicate was an understatement. It wasn't just the past feelings making it awkward. She'd *liked* kissing him. A lot. After months and months of wishing he'd just disappear!

A rueful grin flickered over his face. "I don't mean to."

She sighed, then came over and sat beside him on the step, careful not to let her leg touch his. "Don't say anything to anyone, please? No one knows. And it doesn't matter now, anyway. This was my last chance." She fiddled with a nub of denim on the knee of her jeans.

"What do you mean, your last chance? One, who have you been seeing? He can't be from Cadence Creek, and you're always working, so when have you had time to date? And two, you're not even thirty. You have lots of time to have babies. You'll probably get married again, you know?"

"I don't want to get married again. Ever."

Her voice was flat and definite.

"Aw, come on. Forever is a long time."

She angled him a sideways look. "Yeah, well, I don't have any burning desire to put myself in a position to be hurt and mocked and lied to again. No, thanks."

"You know not every marriage is like that," he reasoned.

"Well, I've been burned once. I don't think I'm willing to chance it again."

"Maybe you just haven't met the right guy."

The words shouldn't have stung, but they did. They brought back every broken teenage dream she'd had, along with the sledgehammer of painful memories from the divorce. Add to that kissing Coop tonight. Clearly, he didn't categorize himself as "the right guy"—he never had. And as such he never should have kissed her at all.

"I plan on doing this all on my own," she explained, her tone a little sharp. "I haven't been seeing anyone besides the lovely people at the clinic in Edmonton. Flying solo."

He sat back. "Are you saying you've been going to a sperm bank?"

She nodded. "It's called intrauterine insemination. This was my third try. I was really hoping it would take this time. I don't have much in savings and I won't borrow against the shop."

He let out a huge breath. "So the crying and running from the party…"

"I was a few days late. I got hopeful that this time was it. I even wished on that stupid star the night you walked me home. And…"

She let the rest of that sentence hang. They'd worked through a bunch of stuff that night. Now she half wished he'd just left her alone. Of course, the other half was still sighing blissfully, remembering the magic of his lips just now.

"But why? Why now?"

She tucked her hands between her knees. "I always wanted kids. When my marriage broke up, we'd been trying, with no luck." She looked over at Coop. "You probably knew that."

"No, no I didn't." His gaze met hers. "I didn't know you'd started trying."

"Looking back, I think it was probably more me trying. Or maybe Scott trying and thinking he wouldn't get caught dipping his nib in the company ink. He was more about himself than I ever realized. Oh, what a stupid cliché we were."

Coop sighed. "I always knew he had a good

ego. I didn't think it had developed into such a big sense of entitlement. Not until…"

He didn't have to finish the rest. She sighed. "Scott took everything from me, at least for a while. My marriage, my dream of a family, my self-respect…" She lifted her chin. "I got back my self-respect, and I found a way to support myself. Unfortunately, humans have yet to find a way to reproduce on their own. And the last thing I want to do is marry someone just to have a child. That's ridiculous. So I did what I've been doing since the day I threw his stuff in the front yard. I did it myself."

She sniffed. "At least I tried to. Didn't turn out so great."

Cooper didn't say anything for a long time. She knew it probably sounded crazy to a guy like him. Heck, he was right, they weren't even thirty yet. But he'd never been married, and there were days where she felt about fifty, not twenty-seven.

He dropped his forehead on his hand. "I should have found a way to make Scott see reason," he mumbled. "To make him do the right thing. You should never have been put in this position."

"Do you really think that's accurate? Yes, Coop, I wish you'd told me. But would I want

Scott back? I've had lots of time to think about it and the answer is no. Even if you had convinced him to break things off with her, I realize now that he probably would have done it again. He didn't love me enough. I'd rather he was gone than settle for what he was prepared to give."

"So you're not still in love with him?"

She nearly choked. Almost laughed, but saw that Coop was dead serious. She folded her hands together. "Did you really think that? That I was still in love with him?"

"I'm not sure you ever get over someone you really love."

She hesitated. Coop was hovering too close to a truth she'd suspected for quite some time. "Scott can't hurt me anymore," she whispered. "I promise."

"I'm glad to hear you say that. No one should have to settle, you know?"

"I'd rather be alone than be the woman everyone talks about behind their hands. To be a laughingstock or worse…pitied. Poor Melissa, so oblivious that her husband is sleeping around. I'm well rid of him."

Cooper reached over and took her hand. "For what it's worth, he's the one who should be pitied. Look what he threw away."

Something warm curled within her. This

was the Coop she remembered. Not the physical touching; he'd been careful not to cross that line. But he always knew what to say when things went sideways. He might tease her incessantly, but when the chips were down, he'd been around, and he'd say something to make her feel better.

It was a shame that he had also thrown that away, though by inaction, not by being a sleazebag. At least she could say that for him.

She let him in on a little piece of insight she'd never shared with anyone. "Yeah, well, I know that love-for-a-lifetime thing happens, but I'm not sure it's meant to happen *to me*. Hence, me doing this on my own."

"You're a strong woman, Mel. Stronger than a lot of people give you credit for."

She was surprised and pleased that after the initial shock, he wasn't judging. "I don't know about that. I'm sad, Coop. I really thought this time was it. I pictured putting together a nursery and buying cute baby things and thinking about next summer and the two of us taking walks in the summer sun. I wanted it so much. Now that's not going to happen. I'm just so…disappointed."

"You can't try again?"

She shrugged. "When do you say enough is enough? Four tries? Five? When you start going into debt? There are other options. I'm just not ready to think about them quite yet."

She knew very well that she could start the adoption process. But there was that little part of her that desperately wanted to experience everything about motherhood, including pregnancy. She wanted that rounded belly and the chance to feel her baby kick. She wanted to hear the heartbeat and see the ultrasound picture. She wasn't sure she was ready to let go of that dream yet. She was going to have to let the dust settle and then think about a next step.

"I'm sorry. What are you going to do now?"

"You mean tonight? Or after that? Because I'm not exactly thinking long-term right now. I won't be pursuing the idea for a little while, until I can think things through."

He nodded. "And how about tonight? Are you going to be okay?"

She nodded. "I am now. I'll go inside and uncork the bottle of wine I've been avoiding, you know, just in case. Then I'll get up tomorrow and clean my house and probably go to the shop and get a jump start on Monday's arranging. I've got a shipment coming Monday afternoon, and that'll keep me busy." She truly was feeling better, and she knew Coop was to thank for that. "It helped just to talk about it, you know? Anyway, do you want me to drive you home? Now you're stranded here without a vehicle."

"I can call my parents. One of them will run into town to get me."

"That's silly. It's the least I can do after you talked me off my ledge. I'm fine now." She held up two fingers, like a "scout's honor" sign.

"Then that'd be great," he replied.

This time she slid behind the wheel and moved the seat ahead while he got in the passenger side. The radio provided some sound in the car on the drive out to the Double C.

When Melissa turned off the road and through the iron gates, she sighed. She'd forgotten how impressive the ranch property was. The lane led straight up to a majestic house, flanked by the dark, hulking shapes of barns. Rolling fields extended for acres and acres. When she'd spent time here, she'd always felt as if she had room to breathe. It was wide-open spaces and serenity.

"I haven't been out here for a long time," she remarked. "I kind of forgot how big and beautiful it is."

"I took over the running of it four years ago," Cooper explained. "Though Dad still has a hand in decisions and works around the place whenever he wants."

"No friction between you two?"

He laughed a little. "Not much. We think a lot alike, and I value his wisdom. He's been doing this a long time."

The headlights touched on the main house. It was large and impressive, but the shrubs and garden around it—his mother's handiwork—kept it from seeming cold and impersonal. The front was lit with floodlights, illuminating the beige stucco, white trim and heavy wood door.

"Turn left," he said, pointing to a drive leading away to a smaller structure tucked slightly behind the house. "I'm over there."

She obediently turned. "When did you stop living in the main house?"

He chuckled. "Shortly after I took over and decided it was a bit lame to be living with Mom and Dad at my age. It's not as big, but it's big enough. Couple thousand square feet, four bedrooms."

She stopped the car in front of the two-bay garage. "For that family you haven't started yet?"

Cooper felt a strange mix of feelings at her question. He'd built the house at the same time that she was starting her business. It was his attempt at moving on and starting a new phase after something so painful. And it was strange talking to her about it, considering he'd held a torch for her for so long. Had he really had the asinine thought that this would be about letting go and moving on? The more time he spent with her, the more complicated his thoughts became. Especially after tonight, and finally kissing her the way he'd wanted to for years. It didn't feel like an ending. It felt like a beginning. A beginning where he was walking on a tightrope.

"I do want that someday," he admitted. "I always have."

"Well, I hope you choose better than I did," she answered, putting the car in Park.

She said it so easily, this suggestion about him finding a wife. What clearer indication did he need that she wasn't interested in him? He should get that through his head by now. She only wanted to be friends. Any crush she'd had on him had died when they were sixteen, and the kiss tonight had simply been the result of high emotion. He needed to accept that. She was never going to love him in that way. No, instead she was in love with the idea of being a single mom. Doing it all herself.

So what was he doing, torturing himself by bringing up old history? She didn't want him. Not anymore. And he had enough male pride to be a little put out that she felt better after *talking*. Wasn't that just awesome.

"Thanks for the lift. Drive carefully, okay?"

"I'm fine now."

"You're sure?"

"I'm sure. Thanks for the talk, Coop. I know I've been harsh but…it was almost like old times, you know? I always felt better after talking to you."

Yeah. Just like old times. He'd done a lot of listening about how much she loved Scott. He was one patient, caring SOB.

But he didn't say that. What he said was, "Anytime, Mel. I'm here for you anytime."

He got out and shut the door, then stood in the dark watching her turn around and drive away. Her taillights disappeared down the road and he kicked at the dirt in the driveway.

Damned if he hadn't meant every word. And he knew exactly where that left him.

Screwed. Because right now he was considering something so crazy, so impossible… It was the one way he might be able to finally make up for all the things he'd done wrong. And in order to give her the one thing she wanted most, he would have to let go of any lingering hopes of them ever being together.

CHAPTER SIX

MELISSA DID EXACTLY what she said she would. She went home, uncorked the bottle of wine, unearthed the emergency stash of chocolate and felt sorry for herself. Then she fell into bed, exhausted, and got up the next morning feeling even worse. She swallowed pain relievers with her orange juice to help with the ache in her head and her back, and then cleaned her house until it was spotless. She wanted to forget that the humiliation of last night had ever happened. But to do that, she'd have to forget kissing Coop, and that event was branded into her brain. Every sound, every touch, every taste.

She just had to try harder to put him out of her mind. She went into the shop to do some arranging. It never failed to divert her thoughts as she worked with the different blooms and color combinations. Fall hues were in and she liked working with the asters and mums and carnations, all in cozy orangey-rusts. But after the second cheerful bouquet—this one set in a very traditional cornucopia—went all wrong she knew she might as well give up. Her head wasn't in it today. Neither was her heart.

She knew exactly where it was. It was at the Double C.

She'd been surprised at how she'd opened up to Coop last night. Granted, he'd pressed her into it, but it had come as such a relief to finally just *tell* someone. And he hadn't judged. At least, not much. Maybe because he'd been there when her whole life had gone into the toilet, and he understood the why behind her decision.

Now she was reminded of the friendship they'd shared before. Maybe he'd made a mistake. No, not maybe; he had. But he had also been caught in the middle, trying to do what was right.

Hmm. Was she forgiving him? She thought she had before, but now she wasn't so sure. All she knew was that she wasn't as angry. And that had come with the words she'd uttered last night about not wanting Scott back. She wished she'd found out about her ex-husband's indiscretion a different way, but it would have been far worse to not know and spend years in a sham of a marriage. Her spidey senses told her that his affair wasn't his first and probably wouldn't have been his last. She'd been so wrong…about so many things.

Cooper could never know how affected she'd been by that kiss. How everything had seemed to fade away until all that was left was the sensation of finally being in his arms. Finally knowing exactly what he tasted like, and even more disturbing, realizing that it was somehow familiar, even though it had never happened before. All the hopped-up, tingly sensations today made it feel as if someone had reached in and turned the clock back to age fifteen.

But they weren't love-struck kids anymore. They were adults. They'd been through stuff a lot more serious than not having homework done or losing a football game. More than ever, right now, Mel longed to be somewhere that felt familiar. Someplace like home, a touchstone to a past she'd once known and loved. The iron gates and majestic house at the Double C had sent a flood of familiarity through her last night, even in the dark. Maybe she'd take a drive out there today.

Or not. That was a bit obvious, wasn't it? Resolutely she got out a pumpkin-shaped bowl and inserted a foam core in the center. For several minutes she worked on adding orange lilies, yellow daisies and poms, peachy-orange roses and crimson-veined carnations into a Thanksgiving arrangement. Frowning, she reached for a few spears of wheat and bunches of artificial cranberries just for a teensy pop of color.

She tapped her fingers on the work counter. She liked this one. And yet her mind kept straying to the Double C and Coop. What was he thinking in the clear light of day? People became single parents all the time, but normally because they got caught or their marriage had split. This kind of thing—intrauterine insemination—simply wasn't done in a town the size of Cadence Creek.

Melissa wanted to believe Cooper would keep the information to himself, but what if something like this got out? She had to make sure he understood. She'd been prepared to deal with questions after the fact, but now, when it looked as if pregnancy was a moot point, she'd really rather keep it hush-hush. No sense overturning the apple cart.

And then it hit her—the perfect excuse. She'd never given Coop back his jacket, or Jean back her cookie dish. Mel could drop both off and say thank you for last night. And remind him—very nicely, of course—that he'd promised to keep her secret to himself.

Before she could change her mind, she locked

up the shop and stopped by her house for his jacket and the dish.

The autumn afternoon was gilded in warm sunlight. When Melissa pulled up to the gate, she caught her breath. She hadn't been able to see things quite so clearly last night in the dark, but she'd truly forgotten how stunning the Double C was. What had been dark shapes then were in full, vibrant color today. The house looked like a country club with its white pillars and creamy-beige stucco. Coop's place was smaller but equally as beautiful, with a similar, down-scaled design. To the right and beyond lay the immaculately kept stables and fields where the Fords made their fortune breeding stock horses.

The Double C appeared to be doing even better than before. As she pulled into Coop's yard she paused to watch a pair of chestnuts gallop along a pasture fence, manes and tails streaming. She sighed, watching as one gave a sassy little buck. Coop must love it out here, with all the space and freedom. She felt a bit of pride, knowing her friend was such a success. He'd always been focused and driven. Now he put that attention into the family business, and it was clearly thriving.

She went to the door and knocked. His truck was in the yard, but there was no answer. Mel was heading back to her car when her cell phone vibrated in her pocket. She pulled it out and saw a new text message on her screen.

Watching football at the big house. Come on up.

Her gaze swerved to Jean and Bob's place. A figure stood in a big window facing her way, and as she squinted she saw him wave. With a laugh she tucked the phone back in her pocket, got in her car and drove the short distance to the mansion.

Coop met her at the door. "Hey. This is a surprise."

She held up the jacket and container. "I was at loose ends. I thought I'd finally return your jacket. I forgot last night."

"You're doing okay?"

She shrugged. "Yeah. I guess." It was nice of him to ask. Was she still bummed? Very. But she was giving herself time to settle, not make any rash decisions.

"I thought you were going to go into the shop today."

"I did for a while. I got restless."

He seemed to accept that and stood aside. "Well, you might as well come in. We're just starting the second quarter and there's a rumor that Mom is making nachos at halftime."

"Are you sure? I don't want to intrude."

"I'm sure."

Stepping inside felt familiar, even though she hadn't visited in years. Despite their obvious affluence, the Fords had made their house warm and welcoming, with no pretense or airs. She followed Coop into the den, where his parents sat together on a leather love seat, eyes glued to the screen as the Edmonton Eskimos hit first down and ten.

"Hey, look who I found," Coop said, stepping into the room.

Jean popped up from the love seat immediately. "Melissa! This is a lovely surprise."

"I brought back your dish," she said, holding it out. "I know it's the real deal and figured you'd want it back."

"Are you feeling better? Coop said he drove you home early last night."

Mel smiled, warmed by the concern. And feeling a little let down that she wasn't spending the afternoon with her own parents. She hadn't talked to them in a couple of weeks. "Much better, thank you. A good night's sleep was just what the doctor ordered. I don't mean to intrude on your afternoon, though."

"Don't be silly," Bob said, tearing his eyes from the screen. "It's good to have you around again. Have a seat. We're getting our butts kicked, but there's still time to turn it around."

She sat on the sofa, a different one than she remembered. It really had been a long time since she'd been here. Cooper sat, too, but left the middle cushion between them. She let herself get absorbed in the game for a while, cheering when the quarterback made a great pass, only to have it incomplete. When the kicker missed the next field goal, everyone sat back in disgust.

"I can't watch. I'm going to put those nachos in the oven," Jean said.

"I'm going to grab another beer," Bob added, putting his hands on his knees and getting up. "You want another, Coop? Melissa? Get you anything?"

"I'm fine, thank you," she said, and Coop waved his dad off. As the halftime whistle sounded, they found themselves alone.

"Why'd you really come today, Mel?"

She tucked one ankle beneath her other leg and turned a little on the sofa so she was half facing him. Leave it to Coop to get right to the heart of the matter. "I was trying to put together some arrangements for tomorrow and I couldn't focus. I just needed to get away, get some space, you know? These days my life is going from home to the shop, maybe to the Wagon Wheel or grocery store or post office, and back home again. I needed some room to breathe, I think. Especially if…" She paused. "Well, I can't go on this way indefinitely. I need to figure out what comes next."

"So you came here. To me."

She frowned and looked away. "Gee, don't make it sound like that."

"Like what?"

"Like *that.*"

He persisted. "Like someone who kissed you silly last night?"

Her gaze snapped to his. She didn't want it to, but it was a reflexive response to his question. For a moment tension snapped between them and she remembered his fingers digging into her bottom as he moved into a full-body press last night.

"That shouldn't have happened."

"Why?"

He was undeterred. Mel stole a glance at the archway, but only heard muffled sounds of Bob and Jean talking and the creak of an oven door. No chance of being interrupted yet.

"Because we're barely even friends again. It just confuses everything. And I wanted to make

sure you weren't going to say anything about…
you know."

He gave a snort of disbelief. "You mean about
you trying to get knocked up by some anony-
mous donor with a turkey baster? Don't worry,
my lips are sealed."

She pursed her lips. "That's exactly the reaction I'm trying to avoid. Thanks a lot."

He let out a breath. "Sorry. That wasn't fair.
What you do is your business, Mel. I'm more
annoyed that you think I'd shout it to the roof-
tops or something. You should know me better
than that."

She swallowed. "Fair enough." She looked
down at her hands, which she'd twisted together.
"Coop, about three years ago… I need to get
over that. After all, it wasn't you who cheated
on me. When Scott left, I had to have a place to
put my resentment. I guess I chose you, because
I felt betrayed by you, too."

"I know, and I'm—"

She cut him off. "I know you're sorry. And the
truth is we can't change it now. In some ways I
wouldn't even want to. The last few weeks reminded me of the kind of friends we were before. I've missed that. I guess I'm kind of hoping
you'll forgive me for holding a grudge for so

long. And I'll forgive you for being so snippy just now."

She looked into his eyes. They seemed almost green in the afternoon light, the color brought out by the green in the Eskimos sweatshirt he wore. Coop was so good-looking. He was a good guy deep down, he was successful, and she couldn't imagine why some woman hadn't snapped him up yet.

And he'd kissed her last night.

Remembering caused her to shift her gaze away, back to the television screen. There were ads on, but she didn't register them.

"So you're not interested in me that way," he said, more of a confirmation than a question.

"I'm not interested in anyone that way," she replied. "And besides, it would be a quick way to ruin a friendship."

"Food's up!" Jean called from the kitchen.

For a second Coop looked as if he was going to say something else, but he finally gave a crooked smile and relaxed his shoulders. "What do you think? You up for nachos?"

Mel grinned, relieved he hadn't pressed the issue. "Of course."

They made their way to the kitchen, where Jean had the platter set on the island counter, surrounded by bowls of salsa, sour cream and guacamole. Coop's eyes widened when Melissa pulled several cheese-encrusted chips onto her plate, all topped with jalapeño peppers. For the next several minutes they chatted and laughed, and Melissa helped herself to a can of pop to counter the heat from the peppers and salsa.

The game came back on, but the score got worse when a turnover resulted in a touchdown by the opposing team. When Coop asked if she wanted to go for a walk to stretch their legs, Melissa agreed—especially after eating that many chips and guacamole. The afternoon was warm, so they made do with what they were wearing as they wandered outside, gravitating toward the ranch buildings.

"We've expanded some since you were here last," he said, leading her past the main barn. "Business is good." He pointed at a new structure. "We built an indoor ring, and use it for a lot of training. It's quiet now, because it's Sunday, but it's usually pretty busy, working the horses, training them up. Stu's good around the barns, but I've got a couple of first-class guys who really know what they're doing."

The passion and pride in his voice was unmistakable. "You've got a good reputation," she said, ambling beside him, feeling the warmth of the sun soak into her. "I mean…in business."

He barked out a laugh. "Not so good with the ladies?"

She kept step with him as they made their way down a dirt lane toward a small pasture. "Rumor has it you haven't been too active in the love department lately. Which is funny, because I seem to remember you enjoying female company quite a bit."

He was quiet for several beats, and she turned her head to look up at him, questioning.

"I dated to put in time," he confessed. "So that I wouldn't be the single guy when everyone was pairing up. But I wasn't looking for anything serious."

"So you changed girls like you changed your socks?"

His lips twitched. "It was hardly that often."

"You never dated anyone more than a month or two," she pointed out.

"No, I didn't."

"So why the sudden drop into celibacy?" They'd reached a fence and Mel stepped forward to rest her arms on the white painted rail. "Amy said she asked you out and you turned her down. I think you hurt her pride."

He did laugh then. "Amy seems to manage all right. One of these days she's going to find someone and get her claws in good and tight. I sure didn't want to be that guy."

"She thinks that someone broke your heart."

Coop's gaze pierced Mel. "Since when did I become a hot topic of conversation around Foothills Floral Design?"

"Since you brought me cookies," she confessed.

Instead of responding, he bent forward and gave a low whistle. About a half-dozen heads popped up, ears twitching, and then, as a group, the animals trotted over to the fence, all long legs and soft noses and wide eyes.

"Oh, babies!" Mel smiled widely as the colts and fillies approached the railings. "Oh my goodness, Coop, they're adorable!"

"Aren't they?" He reached through the gap and scratched between the ears of one buckskin colt. "I love them at this age. They're full of oats, you know? All energy and cuteness. And all except for one is spoken for."

"Which one?"

He pointed to a sorrel filly with a white star. "Her. She's from Ford's Firebrand and Morning Mist."

"Misty! Oh my gosh, you still have her?"

He grinned. "Yeah, we still do. I remember she was your favorite. She's fourteen now and has a number of offspring. I wanted one of hers here, you know?"

"You sentimental, Coop?"

He smiled. "Maybe a little." The filly came over to the fence and Mel reached out and rubbed her soft jaw.

"You really love this place, huh."

He nodded. "Always have. It's my heart and soul. The only thing I ever wanted to do was work with Dad and take over the reins when the time came. I learned at his elbow. It's not a job. This is my life, you know?"

"I think I do. It's rare, your connection. I love the flower shop, love what I do and how I've built it. But this…this goes deeper. This is right down to your boots, isn't it?"

"It is. The land, the horses, breeding them, training them…I can't imagine doing anything else."

She was quiet for a moment as the horses drifted away, and then she sighed. "Can I make a confession, Coop?"

He chuckled. "Why not? Hate for you to stop now."

She gripped the fence and stared at the fields beyond the small pasture. "How you feel about this place? That's how I feel about having a family. It's like there's a part of me that's missing.

I'm proud of how I got back on my feet after the divorce. I love that I've made a go of my own business and I enjoy the business I chose. It's not that I'm unhappy. But there's a part of me that wants—needs—to be a mother. I can feel it in the deepest part of me, you know?"

She looked at him and raised her eyebrows, asking the question that had bugged her more than anything the last months. "Does that make me less of an independent woman, do you think?"

Coop reached over and put his hand on top of hers. "Of course not. What makes you strong and independent is making choices that are right for you no matter what anyone else thinks. Following your heart and doing what it takes to make your dreams a reality. And you know this, right? Believe me, Mel, having a career and being a mom are not mutually exclusive events. I know people don't realize it, because she was always here, but my mom was—is—a fantastic parent, yet she also put in countless hours on the ranch. She's always kept all the books and records, and wasn't afraid to get her boots dirty, either."

"So you don't think less of me for what I've been trying to do?"

Coop chuckled and slid his hand away. Melissa missed the feel of it, warm and reassuring, on top of hers. Just weeks ago she couldn't stand the sight of him. But maybe the time had been right to let go of old grudges.

"Was I surprised at last night's revelation? You bet. Who wouldn't be? I can just imagine what the women in town would say if they knew."

"Probably something very similar to what you said inside," Mel admitted.

"It's just not how we do it here in the Creek. But I don't think less of you, of course not. I'm a little in awe, to be honest. It's a brave thing to step outside a comfort zone and take a chance, especially knowing what people will say."

The backs of her eyes stung a little. "Thank you for that."

"You're welcome." He grinned. "For the record? You were fierce when you caught Scott with his hand in the proverbial cookie jar. When you put your mind to something, you don't mess around. If this is what you want, you'll find a way."

A flock of magpies chattered in the barnyard, the cacophony filling the silence. Finally, Coop spoke again. "So what's the plan now?"

She knew he was referring to her plans for motherhood. "I'm taking a bit of time to think.

I'm probably going to look into getting on the adoption registry. It wasn't my first choice. I wanted to experience carrying a baby, you know? Feeling the first kicks, buying maternity clothes, going through childbirth classes…"

"Morning sickness, weight gain, labor?"

She laughed. "Those, too. They come with the package." Suddenly the emotion that she'd managed to keep at bay all day came flooding back. "I want to feel my baby stick its toes in my ribs. To go to the doctor and hear the heartbeat, see the ultrasound picture. I want that experience, Coop. If I can't have it, so be it. Like I said, I can't afford to go through IUI attempts indefinitely. And I absolutely refuse to take my mother's advice."

"Which is?"

Mel made a disgusted sound. "Get married. I don't plan on doing that again, but if I did, I would have to be in love with that person, utterly and completely. I couldn't marry someone just to have a baby. I'd far rather my child be brought up by a single mom than in a home where the parents didn't truly love each other."

Which was why, though she hadn't breathed a word of it to anyone, she'd been secretly relieved when she'd gotten her period after Scott had left. If there'd been a baby on the way it might have changed things. It definitely would have complicated them. She would have been tied to him forever, with a child between them. He might have tried to convince her to give their marriage another go. Sometimes in the back of her mind she wondered if that feeling of relief had jinxed her from future success. But then she dismissed it. Wishing on stars was fine but people made their own luck.

"You're going to be a great mom, no question. And who knows? Maybe someday you'll find the right guy."

She swallowed. She'd found him already, when she was fourteen. That ship had sailed. She already knew what it was like to be caught in a marriage that wasn't built on the real thing. Oh, she'd done a good job of lying to herself, but she knew the truth. She'd never loved Scott the way she should have. Maybe that's why she hadn't fought harder to keep him.

And he hadn't loved her completely, either. Otherwise he would have been faithful.

She swallowed against a thick lump in her throat. Together, she and Scott had made a mess of everything, hadn't they? They'd been too young, too foolish.

"Mel?"

"Hmm?" Coop's voice pulled her out of her musings.

"I've been doing a lot of thinking since last night. What would you say if I told you I have a solution to your problem?"

"A solution? I don't follow."

He turned away from the fence and faced her with an intense gaze. His whole demeanor was sober, telling her that whatever was coming next was really important. She didn't know why, but a heaviness that felt like a warning began a slow slide through her body, landing in her stomach.

He picked up her hand. "What if *I* helped you have a baby?"

CHAPTER SEVEN

MEL STARED AT HIM, wondering if she'd heard him correctly. What he was suggesting was preposterous. And yet the steely look in his eye told her he meant every syllable.

"Cooper, that's ridiculous." She felt as if the blood rushed out of her body as she ripped her hand away. Oh, she never should have confided in him last night! She'd grieved a little and then told herself she simply had to move ahead with the next plan. The last thing she needed was Coop breathing life into the old dream again.

Not to mention this was *Coop*. The whole idea was fraught with so many problems she wasn't sure she could count them all.

"It's not ridiculous. For heaven's sake, Mel, who knows you better than I do? Look, I feel partially responsible for your life blowing up in the first place. This could make things right. I know you'll be a fantastic mom."

She drew back, and her gaze shifted from

surprise to suspicion. "Is that what this is? Redemption for you? A way to make you feel better? Because if that's the case, I don't want it."

His brow wrinkled. "Don't call it redemption. What I did was wrong, and I've regretted it every day since. Maybe this is a way to make amends. You want to be a mom. Why shouldn't I help if I'm able? Isn't that what friends do? Help each other?"

Help? She was almost scared to ask the next question, but knew she had to. Cautiously, she looked up at him. "What exactly are you offering, Coop? Because this sounds a little above and beyond the requirements of *friends*."

"To be the father of your baby."

She needed to sit down. The blood rushed out of her head and she felt strangely light. In the absence of any place to sit she held on to the fence rail, gripping the wood with white knuckles.

For a split second she had thought that perhaps he was just going to offer her money to continue trying the treatments. But no, he'd actually said the word *father*.

"Before you freak out, just listen to me," he pressed. "I thought about this all last night. Wouldn't it be better to know who the father of your child is? I mean, you know me, my family, where I come from. Heck, you'd have my genetic history, for that matter. Isn't that better than some stranger from a lab?"

She had to admit that she'd had qualms about not really knowing the donor. There were benefits to that sort of anonymity and there were drawbacks. Any details she saw on paper told her nothing about the man behind the profile. What was he like? Was he a hard worker, funny, kind? Did he like to read or go to movies, did he like the outdoors or was he more of an urban jungle type? And here was Coop. Hardworking, handsome, healthy Coop. Offering to be her baby daddy.

Not in a million years had she seen this coming. The very idea seemed to suck the air clean out of her lungs.

"You haven't really thought about this," she began cautiously. This was a disaster in the making and she knew it. Yet a part of her hummed with hope. What he was offering was a chance. A way to not give up the idea of having her own child.

But with Coop… She gazed up at him. He shouldn't look different than he had only moments before, but he did. She suddenly noticed the way his chest and shoulders filled out his Edmonton Eskimos sweatshirt. The narrowness of his hips and long legs, and the way his jeans seemed to show off his assets to best advantage. She saw his strong, sexy jaw, smoldering eyes and thick, dark hair. And she wasn't just cataloging his features in genetic terms. It was a deep down, visceral acknowledgment that Coop was incredibly good-looking, rugged and fit.

Cooper was gorgeous. And oh, she could just imagine that he'd make gorgeous babies.

On the heels of her assessment came a lightning strike of images so intense that she bit down on her lip. Making a baby with Coop, the traditional way...

She cleared her throat. "Um, how exactly did you see this happening?" she asked. She heard the wobble of nerves in her voice and felt like an idiot. But really, how was one *supposed* to talk about this kind of thing? It was the strangest conversation, with a plethora of land mines to sidestep. "I mean, did you think we...or would you..."

She was so embarrassed. She half hoped the ground would open up and swallow her.

"Would we—" God, his voice was soft as silk "—go about it the usual way?"

She looked up and nodded.

His expression stayed exactly the same—unreadable—as he answered her query with one of his own. "Would you want to?"

Let me die right now.

Again with the images. She was not thinking about sleeping with Coop. She was not.

Only she was. At fifteen she'd dreamed about kissing him. It had been angsty and innocent. At twenty-seven, it was completely different. And that was exactly why it couldn't happen.

"No," she replied, though she suspected she didn't sound very convincing.

"I could be your donor," he said quietly.

Melissa tried to make sense of all the thoughts running through her brain. When she'd thought about coming out here today it had been to escape the noise in her head. To let go of what had been, and to clear a space for thinking about the next step. This was all too much.

She looked around. The sun was still shining, though dropping a little lower in the sky as the afternoon waned. The birds still chattered, the horses grazed, foals frolicked in the pasture— nothing had changed. And yet everything had changed. It had all shifted with his crazy offer to give her the one thing she wanted most.

"And what about the baby?" Her heart lodged in her throat as she asked. "You're prepared to be a sperm donor? Because I'm not looking for any personal entanglements, Coop. How do you see your role in this…after?"

My word, was she actually considering it?

"The baby would be yours, of course," he said calmly, coming forward and taking her hands. "I want to do this for you, Mel. One…friend to another."

As he held her hands she was reminded of how he'd kissed her last night, and the brief flare of passion that had erupted between them. She'd been unable to stop the rush of desire at the touch of his lips on hers. Whether they admitted it or not, there was now this *thing* between them, muddying the waters.

Besides, she knew Coop. She knew him probably better than anyone else on the planet. He would never be satisfied with fathering a child and then stepping back as if it had never happened. Especially in a town this size, where their presence would be front and center every day. He wouldn't be one to stand on the sidelines while his son or daughter grew up, started school, learned to ride a bike…. It simply wasn't in Cooper's DNA and she knew it.

She tried to imagine what a child of theirs might look like, and her heart lurched. Hazel eyes like Coop. Maybe her hair, her nose. She closed her eyes. Coop's smile.

"Don't answer now," he said, letting go of her hands. "Take some time to think about it. It's a big decision. Just know that I'm here, and I'll help you any way I can."

She couldn't speak past the lump in her throat, so she nodded. The fact that he'd even offered…

"Listen, I don't know what your parents have planned, but we're doing our Thanksgiving dinner next Monday. Why don't you join us? Dad's going to try deep-frying the turkey this year. And Mom's guaranteed to have pumpkin pie."

"My parents are still going to be on their New England trip," Melissa admitted. "I don't have plans."

"Then you should definitely come. Maybe we can saddle up Misty for you and we can go for a ride after dinner. And you can tell me what you've decided."

She couldn't deny that there was a part of her that understood the logic behind his offer. And he was right about one thing—she should take time to think it over before she made a final decision. "That might be nice," she answered weakly.

They turned from the pasture and began walking back to the house. They passed the barn, where a couple of the hired hands were doing evening chores. The sound of laughter and shuffling hooves echoed through the open doors, and Coop lifted a hand in greeting to one worker as they passed.

They finally paused by Melissa's car. Coop shifted his weight as she put her hand on the door handle, knowing she should open it, but not quite wanting the afternoon to end. It had been so great—being included in the game and snacks, seeing the babies in the pasture, the warm afternoon. Even Coop's unorthodox suggestion didn't take away from the fact that she'd felt very welcomed and included. Maybe too included.

But it wasn't just that. She didn't want to leave him. It wasn't a new sensation, but it was one she hadn't felt in a very long time. Not since she was a twitterpated teenager and she'd hoped, prayed every night, that one day Cooper would see her as a girl and not just a buddy. She'd spent hours daydreaming about a moment when he'd reach over and twine his fingers with hers, or slide forward that little bit and kiss her like a boy was supposed to kiss a girl. She'd wanted to be his—to wear his jacket and hold his hand and be the one to sit next to him in a booth at the Wagon Wheel, sharing a milkshake after a football game.

She'd waited…and waited…and waited. And

then Scott had come along and offered her all the things that Coop had not.

That weightless, nervous anticipation was swirling within her right now, though. And all it had taken was one kiss, followed by a not-so-simple suggestion about making babies, to put it back in her head.

"I need to think," she whispered, tugging on the door handle. "There's a lot to think about."

"You do that," he answered. "I'll be here. I'm not going anywhere."

For some reason she felt a flicker of anger at the words. No, Cooper wasn't going anywhere. He was as solid as the day was long. He was practically a saint in this town—a good boss, generous with his time, good-looking and affluent. He was damned near perfect.

And it had only taken him all these years to kiss her, and just because she was an emotional wreck. And now he was suggesting something incredibly amazing—but only as her friend, not as her lover.

"Why can't I shake the feeling that you're trying to buy your way back into my life?"

He shoved his hands in his pockets, but his brows puckered as if he was annoyed. "I'm not proud of what my past actions say about me. Maybe I *am* trying to make up for that. If that's looking for redemption, so be it. Is it so wrong for me to want you to be happy?"

"It's just such an abrupt change...."

"Guilt kept me away for a long time. That and the way you looked at me with daggers in your eyes. I figured it had gone on long enough."

She blinked, out of responses. Got behind the wheel and turned the key in the ignition. "See you at Thanksgiving," she said through the open window, and he lifted a hand and waved as she drove off.

It wasn't until she hit the main road that she felt the urge to cry. She didn't, though. She forced herself to remain dry-eyed and steely jawed the entire time. But inside, the feelings were there. It was so obvious and hurtful.

It was the reason why she was so sure she would never marry. The one man who should have loved her hadn't, and the one man she'd always wanted to love her never would.

Having Coop's baby was out of the question. Because being in his life was not at all the same as sharing it, and only a foolish woman would put herself in that position.

Coop plopped his hat back on his head, grabbed his oilskin from the peg and shoved his arms in the sleeves as he made his way out the door.

A cold front over the mountains had dropped a mere half inch of snow on the ground, and it had already disappeared as the precipitation turned to rain. But the rain was cold, and he still had hours of work to get through yet. The farrier was here, and one of the trainers, Luke, was down with the flu. Stu was helping work the horses today, but Coop knew that in just a few days a client would be making his way up from Montana expecting to pick up four horses. They were damned well going to be ready and worthy of coming out of Double C.

He turned up the collar of his jacket against the bitter rain and lowered his chin as he made his way to the barn.

No doubt about it, the rain wasn't helping his mood any. But then, he'd been a bit grouchy ever since he'd offered to be the father of Mel's baby.

It had seemed like a good idea at the time. He understood her reasoning, even if he did think she was being a bit hasty. It also killed him to see her hurting, especially after all she'd been through. If she truly was determined to go through with this—and he could see that she was—he wanted to help.

And that was the problem, wasn't it? He side-stepped a puddle and cursed under his breath. He would go to the moon for her. The only reason he'd stayed away so long was because he knew she had a right to be angry with him, and he'd wanted to give her space.

It had all changed when he'd kissed her. He'd lost his edge, the upper hand. It had made him weak. Willing to accept her friendship on whatever terms she offered. And wasn't that a sure way to get hurt.

Light glowed from the barn windows and he pulled on the sliding door, anxious to get out of the wet. Yes, kissing her had been a mistake. And so had asking her if she wanted to go about things the "usual" way. Because while Scott had been wrong about Coop trying to split them up, he was dead right about Coop's feelings.

If he told her everything about the night he'd confronted Scott, she'd finally understand the real reason he'd acted the way he had. But she would also wonder if his offer to be her donor was his way of making his move, insinuating himself into her life.

And while that hadn't been his initial intent, he wondered that himself. Spilling his guts would take the tenuous trust they'd built lately and crush it to dust. And yet going on without telling her the truth was unthinkable. If nothing else, they had to reestablish their friendship with

total honesty. Lack of honesty had been what
had driven them apart in the first place.

He shut the door behind him and shook the
water off his hat and shoulders. Maybe it was
time he stopped letting his feelings for Mel make
him look like a fool. But if he hadn't figured out
how to do that in ten years, he wasn't too con-
fident in his chances now, either.

Thanksgiving Monday came smack in the middle of a Chinook. The cloud arch formed to the
west, cutting the sky in a precise arc, and the
westerly wind was mild, bringing back an echo
of summer. Mel was surprised to see extra cars
already parked at the Ford house. For a moment
she considered scooting away and then calling
and making her apologies.

Instead she reached back into her car for the
flower arrangement she'd brought, as well as a
long, rectangular gift bag containing a bottle
of wine. Why should she be alone today? The
idea of roasting a single turkey breast and making boxed stuffing for herself sounded horrible.
Especially when she had a perfectly good invitation.

She rang the bell and wished she had a free
hand to run over her hair. She'd put it up in a
simple twist, but was sure the blustery Chinook

wind was ripping it to shreds. A piece flew free and stuck to her lipstick. Perfect. She was already unspeakably nervous about today, about seeing Coop again. To let him know her decision. She'd done nothing but think about it since the last time they spoke.

The door opened and Cooper stood there, dressed in jeans and a starchy-looking red plaid shirt, the front of his body covered by a cotton apron with the words Mr. Good-Lookin' Is Cookin' emblazoned on the front.

"You came."

"You thought I wouldn't?"

He grinned. It made the corners of his eyes crinkle and chased away some of her nerves, filling her with warmth and gladness. "I wondered if you'd turn coward."

"Shows what you know," she retorted, but she was smiling. "Do you suppose I could come in?"

"Oh, sure. Sorry."

He stood aside and she stepped into the foyer. Voices echoed from the kitchen and then there was loud laughter. "Uncle Jason is here with Aunt Sheila, and so is Aunt Rae. It won't be a quiet dinner."

Mel was thinking that was just fine. It would save awkward conversations and she could melt into the background a little. But then she stepped into the kitchen and was immediately pounced on by Bob, who was feeling rather jovial—perhaps after a predinner cocktail.

"Look who's here! I don't know what's prettier, those flowers or the roses in your cheeks."

So much for blending in.

She put the flowers down on the end of the island and couldn't help but chuckle. Bob was dressed similarly to Coop, only his apron boasted a picture of a bull and the message Aged to Perfection.

"Nice," she commented. "But if you two are cooking, I'm not sure I want to stay."

Coop pressed a hand to his heart. "Oh, you wound me!"

Jean came from the pantry with a jar of pickles in her hand. "They're under my direct supervision, Melissa. Don't you worry." She came forward and kissed Mel's cheek. "Glad you could make it. Coop will be on his best behavior."

"I highly doubt that."

Like Coop and Bob, Jean had on an apron, too. It seemed this was a family tradition. And in typical rodeo queen fashion, the former barrel racing champ had on a pink apron with the caption Barrel Racer, Cowboy Chaser.

The aunts and uncle were out on the back deck enjoying a drink. Mel handed over the bottle of wine and asked Jean, "Is there anything I can do to help?"

"Not at the moment. Oh, Melissa, did you bring those flowers? Of course you did. They're gorgeous!" She fussed over the arrangement, a bigger version of the one Mel had created just over a week ago at her shop.

"It was no trouble."

"You've got such a talent." Jean moved the flowers to the dining room, putting them in the center of the table and moving the candles to either side. "You were a real smart cookie, starting up that business."

"Thanks."

Jean paused in the doorway to the dining room, close to Melissa. She reached out and put her fingers lightly on Mel's arm. "We were so sorry when…well, when things weren't going so great for you. But you picked yourself up again and got back in the saddle, and we're real proud of you. We probably should have said it before, but we knew you and Coop…" She colored a little. "Well. You know."

"It's okay. I'm glad you told me now."

"We're just glad you and Coop are…well." She laughed. "I'm usually not so bad at putting words together. Anyway, you were always good friends and it's nice to see you bury the hatchet.

And not in his back. Not that he didn't deserve it. He should have told you what was going on."

"You knew he knew?" All this time Melissa had been under the impression that they'd been in the dark about Coop's involvement.

"Oh, not at the time. He told us one day ages ago when we asked why you weren't friends anymore. Anyway, water under the bridge and all that. How about I fix you a drink? Pumpkin lattes are the warm-up beverage of the day."

"That sounds lovely," Mel replied, already warmed by Jean's awkward but welcoming speech.

The drink was delicious, blending coffee, pumpkin, spice and cream with a dash of toffee liqueur that made it taste more like a dessert than a cocktail. The kitchen smelled of roasting turkey and savory and sage from the stuffing. Everyone sat in the sun on the deck for a little while until Jean went inside to put on the vegetables. Mel offered to help and Coop's mother insisted she wear an apron so she didn't get anything on her good clothing.

She slid the loop over her neck and tied the strings behind her back, then looked down and burst out laughing.

"It's mine," Jean said with a grin.

It said Cowgirls Ride the Hide.

"Let me guess, you collect them?"

"I have a whole drawer full. It's kind of a tradition now. They usually show up in Christmas stockings."

Together they turned the burners on beneath the vegetables, took the turkey out of the oven to rest before carving, and put the brussels sprouts in to roast.

While Jean uncorked a bottle of wine, Mel spooned cranberry sauce and pickles into bowls and placed them on the table. She sliced and buttered fresh buns and arranged them in a wicker basket, and filled water glasses while Jean went to work whipping cream for the pumpkin and pecan pies. The sprouts came out of the oven, the carrots were drained and the potatoes mashed. Bob came in and carved the turkey, and the aunts poured wine and carried bowls to the table while Coop got a lighter and lit the candles flanking Mel's flowers.

And then they all finally sat down at the table, Bob at one end and Coop at the other, Jean at Bob's right elbow and Mel on Coop's, with the aunts and uncle rounding out the sides. Mel tried not to notice that she was seated in the mirror position of Jean and Bob, though she and Coop were not a couple. And yet, as they took their seats, her knee bumped his beneath the table and something exciting shot up her leg. Oh boy.

"Cooper, won't you give a toast?" Jean asked.

Coop raised his glass, then waited until all the glasses were lifted before he said, "To family, to friends, being together and our many blessings. Happy Thanksgiving."

The sound of tinkling crystal echoed in the dining room, and Coop leaned slightly sideways and touched his glass to Melissa's. "Happy Thanksgiving," he said quietly, meeting her gaze.

She was so used to him teasing, to seeing the twinkle in his eyes, that she was quite mesmerized by the soft, serious quality she found there. "To you, too," she replied, and that swirly feeling intensified as they each took a sip of their wine with their gazes locked.

Coop's suggestion echoed in her mind: *The usual way? Would you want to?*

Yes, she thought. Oh yes, she would. And wasn't that a huge surprise. Because ever since Scott left she hadn't felt any burning desire to get caught up in someone that way. Especially Coop. She dropped her eyes to her plate, hoping her thoughts weren't reflected in her gaze. Something her mother always said kept nagging at her, too. She'd always claimed that hate was as passionate an emotion as love. And Melissa had hated Coop for a long time, until it became a habit. Now she was beginning to realize that she hadn't really hated him. She'd had a whole bunch of other emotions where Coop was concerned, hurt and betrayal that had been devastating. She'd called it hate because that had been easier than dealing with her true feelings.

"Mel? Potatoes are to you." Coop nudged her hand with the bowl and she wondered how long he'd been holding them, waiting for her.

"Oh. Thanks."

She made a point of filling her plate and eating, always aware of Coop on her left. He laughed and smiled a lot, teasing his family and getting as good as he got. He'd taken off the silly apron and had rolled up his sleeves. She noticed he wore a watch but no other jewelry, no rings, no nothing.

Coop, she realized, hadn't changed that much at all. He was still a no-fuss kind of guy who didn't feel the need to put on a show. But then, he didn't need to, did he? He was the kind of man who seemed to command attention without even trying.

"More wine, Mel?"

She looked up at him. He was holding the bottle and waiting for her response. She shook her head. "I probably shouldn't. Not after that dessert masked as a cocktail earlier. I have to drive later."

He put down the bottle. "We still on for that ride?"

The meal was delicious, but at his question her appetite started to fade. So far this afternoon she'd ignored the fact that later on they were going to have an uncomfortable conversation.

"Why not? I haven't ridden for a long time. It's a good day for it."

"Give us a chance to work off dinner," he added.

"No kidding. I haven't had a turkey dinner with all the trimmings since last Christmas at Mom's. I almost had to roll myself home. I can't eat like I could when I was sixteen anymore. I look at a meal like this and gain five pounds."

His gaze swept over her. "Naw, I doubt it. You look as good as you always did, Mel."

Her cheeks warmed and his leg brushed hers again. Whether it was intentional or by accident, the ripples still felt the same. Oh, she'd definitely made the right decision. Finding the right way to tell him, though—that was going to be a real challenge.

When the main meal was over, Mel joined the women in clearing the table of plates and then serving pie and coffee. She was slicing into the pecan pie when Coop stepped up behind her and put his hand over hers on the knife, sliding it farther to the right to make the piece bigger. "That's about right," he said.

His breath was warm on her ear, his body close behind her so that if she backed up even an inch, her spine would be pressed against his broad chest. She swallowed and told herself to breathe normally. "Are you sure you don't want a smaller one so you can have a piece of each?"

He leaned in closer. "I'll let you in on a little secret." His lips brushed her ear. "There's a second pumpkin pie hidden in the fridge for later."

She shivered. And she knew he knew, because she felt his lips curve in a smile against her ear.

She shrugged him away. "Oh, stop pestering me and let me cut the pie, or else you won't get any!"

"You tell him, Mel!" Bob cheered her on and Aunt Rae laughed beside her.

"Get on with you, Cooper," Aunt Rae chided. "You always were a torment. I'm with Melissa on this one."

He took his piece of pie and got a scoop of whipped cream for the top from his mother, then left the kitchen for the comfort of the dining room again.

But Melissa couldn't help feeling as if the family was pairing them up today, and Cooper's actions did nothing to deter that line of thinking. And that simply couldn't happen. A guy like Cooper flirted without even realizing it. It was second nature to him; she'd seen him turn that smile on girls for as long as she'd known him. It annoyed her a lot that she wasn't any more immune than those other girls had been.

But it ended here. He didn't really mean it. He never did. And it was why there couldn't be anything between them, and exactly the reason he could never be the father of her child. In the end she'd be the one to pay. She'd start to care too much and she'd be the one hurt.

Once was enough for that, thank you very much.

CHAPTER EIGHT

SHE NEARLY BACKED OUT of the plans to go riding, but doing so would put her in an awkward position. Granted, she hadn't had a lot to drink at dinner, but she'd had the latte and then a full glass of wine, and wasn't quite sure she should drive yet. The dishes had been put in the dishwasher and the aunts had insisted on washing up the rest as Mel and Jean finished clearing the table. When Cooper said they planned to go riding, they'd practically been shooed out the door.

Now Melissa was astride Misty and finding it hard to be sorry. When they'd been kids, they'd gone riding a lot. Misty had been younger then and full of beans, as Bob used to say. But he'd trusted Mel with her, and while Melissa's equestrian skills were rusty now, it all felt very familiar as she relaxed in the saddle and held the reins easily in her hands.

"Where to?" Coop asked. He was astride Sergeant, a ten-year-old sorrel stallion with strong hindquarters and a wide, muscled chest. The horse tossed his head a little, his mane shivering in the wind, and danced a bit to the side. Without breaking his gaze from Mel, Coop settled the animal with barely a movement of his body or hands.

"Up to you," she replied. There were tons of places on the ranch. They could head east and wind their way along the creek to the butte, or north past the pastures and on to the slough, where there was shelter in the trees. Or they could follow the creek the other way, down into the gulley.

"Let's go west," he suggested. "Then we'll have the wind at our back on the way home."

He led the way and she couldn't help but admire the figure he made in the saddle. He was all long legs and lean hips, with a perfectly straight back and relaxed, wide shoulders. He'd put on his jean jacket again and when he turned his head to follow the path of a flock of geese, the brim of his hat nearly touched the collar. Once they were out of the yard, Coop looked back and grinned, and then nudged Sergeant into a canter. The speed was nothing Mel couldn't handle, and she settled into the rocking gait easily. He was letting the horses get some exercise, and it was fun, too. She caught up to him and moved alongside, then gave Misty a nudge and opened her up to a gallop. She heard Coop's laugh behind her, but only for a short while. In no time he'd brought the stallion forward and they rode neck and neck, heading nowhere fast and loving every minute.

Before long they reached the narrow, snaking creek and slowed to a trot, then a walk. They rode beside it for a long time until a narrow path appeared, leading down into the secluded gulley.

The rock along the creek bed was multicolored, a unique striation of geological layers that had been formed over millions of years. The Chinook wind didn't reach the sheltered canyon, and the creek meandered through, unhurried on this lazy autumn day.

Coop halted his horse at a particularly wide spot and dismounted, letting Sergeant walk forward to get a drink from the cool creek. Mel followed suit, her hand loosely on the reins as Misty dipped her nose in the water. Instead of mounting up again, Coop grabbed Sergeant's reins and started walking, leading him along the creek.

They kept on, silent, until they reached a small stand of trees just barely hanging on to their bright yellow leaves. Coop looped the reins around a branch and then secured Misty as well.

Then he held out his hand to Melissa and said simply, "Walk with me."

She hesitated. Coop's hand was still there, waiting for her to take it, and she wanted to and was afraid to all at once. Didn't he realize he was playing with her feelings here? And yet… it was only holding hands, and she was twenty-seven years old. Maybe she was making far too much of things.

She put her palm against his and his fingers tightened around hers.

They didn't go far, just ambled up the creek a little. The stream burbled and whispered over rocks strewn on the bottom, and Coop's steps were slow and lazy. When Mel felt they had to say something or she would surely burst, he paused, turned to face her and said, "I'm sorry, Mel. I can't wait to do this any longer."

Her lips were still open with surprise when his mouth came crashing down on hers. Oh glory, he tasted good. Like rich coffee and sweet brown sugar and one hundred percent man. Every rational thought she possessed, every rehearsed line she'd practiced in her head, was pushed out by the reality that was Cooper. She did the only thing she could in the moment—she responded. She kissed him back, planting her booted feet in the gravel and gripping the shoulders of his jacket to pull him closer.

He leaned his weight against her, forcing her to take a step backward. She nearly lost her balance when she realized he was guiding her, pushing her step by step to the rock wall that kept them secluded from the rest of the world. The cold, smooth surface touched her shoulder blades, supporting her weight, and still Coop's mouth made its magic against hers. Her eyes were closed and every nerve ending in her body was at full attention. It would be so easy to let go. To lose control. It had been so long....

But Coop's urgency grew tempered and his kiss gentled. Instead of relieving the tension, that magnified it by about a hundred. Now it was slow. Seductive. And very, very deliberate. His touch was full of nuances, from the tiny nudge encouraging her to open her mouth wider, to the brush of his hand over her hip, to the delicious sound of pleasure that rumbled in his throat. Never in her life had Mel completely understood what girls meant when they said they melted into a puddle, but she did now. If not for the rock behind her and Coop's body bracing her against it, she was relatively sure that her boneless body would collapse into a blissful heap of arousal.

"I could do this forever," he murmured against her cheek.

"Oh please, no," she replied breathlessly. "I'm fairly sure I couldn't survive that long."

"Without what?" His teeth nibbled at her ear.

"Without..." She lost her train of thought as he nipped at her neck, then slid his lips back to her mouth, where he kissed the sensitive corner. "Oh *God,* Coop."

"You, too, right?" Somewhere in the last few minutes his hat had come off, and he pressed his forehead to hers. "It's not just me. Say it's not just me."

"It's not just you."

"I don't want to stop. I don't think I can stop touching you."

It had been a very long time since someone had said something like that to her, and meant it. She gloried in the sensation of being wanted and craved. As much as she knew there were other things at stake, she wanted just a few more minutes. She could stop thinking for a few more minutes, right?

His mouth fused with hers again, their bodies so twined together that there came a point where they had to either start removing clothing or step away. It was a point of no return, and for the space of a few seconds Mel considered all the possibilities. All of them.

To her surprise, it was Coop who stepped back first. He stopped, looked into her eyes and said something incredibly pithy and profane before turning away. She took it as a very heartfelt compliment. For a woman who'd been made to feel undesirable and inadequate, it was a definite score for her feminine pride.

She waited, trying to rein in her reeling senses. Coop stood on the edge of the creek with his back to her, his shoulders rising and falling as he caught his breath.

Was it really just a week ago he'd offered to help her have a baby?

It was impossible to reconcile the two ideas. Impossible to think of Coop as nothing more than a sperm donor. And impossible to think of making love to him. Oh, she could envision that well enough, but how it would fit into her life didn't compute. She could never just have sex for sex's sake, not with Coop. And she really couldn't comprehend it ever being more than that. It was too big. Too...scary.

They were in such a pickle.

She stepped over the gravel, her boots crunching in the silence. She was nearly to his shoulder when he said, in a low, ominous voice, "The answer was always going to be no, wasn't it?"

It stopped her in her tracks. "I'm afraid so, Coop. I just can't."

She studied his profile. His jaw tightened, and his back was ramrod straight. Without looking at her, he spoke. "I don't suppose I'm ever going to be good enough for you, right?"

"What?" She stepped forward and grabbed his arm. "Where the heck did that come from? I have several reasons for saying no, Coop, but not one of them has anything to do with you being good enough for me! Wow."

"But you'd have some random stranger—or no baby at all, before letting me be the father."

There was such bitterness in his voice, and she wondered where it came from. "Oh, for Pete's sake. You men, it's always about your damned pride, isn't it? You want reasons, Coop?"

She started ticking them off on her fingers. "First of all, you say that this would be my baby, but I know you. You theoretically wouldn't want to be involved, but you wouldn't be able to help yourself. I'm not looking for a parenting partner. Secondly, if I did go ahead with it, knowing this was your baby, how could I possibly deny you access to your child? And before you say it, I know, just as you do, that you want a family and kids of your own. Once he or she was here… Like I said, you wouldn't be able to help yourself."

She touched a third finger. "This is a small town. The secret would get out. Even if we kept it quiet, what if our kid looked like you? Oh, the speculation! The last thing I want is my child being brought up with whispers about whether or not someone local is his real father. I've had my share of whispers behind my back, believe me."

She lowered her hand. "But more than all of those reasons, Coop, is this. You and me. This would tie us to each other forever in ways I'm certainly not prepared for. We're barely even friends again. Parents? And then there's…what happened today. Everything is mixed up. We've got no business bringing a baby into the middle of that. It's just better if I…if I do this alone."

Today had changed the game, though. Suddenly "alone" sounded awfully empty. And how would it feel to carry another man's child, knowing that Coop was out there, with his great kisses and sexy smile and…

She sighed. And what? Oh, why did he have to come along and complicate everything?

Coop faced her. "After today, do you think

I could stand to see you carry another man's child? Do you know what that would do to me?"

Confused, she frowned. "Do to you? It got pretty hot, pretty fast, but it wasn't more than a couple of kisses, really. I mean…all our clothes stayed where they belonged."

"You tell yourself that," he said darkly, his eyes glittering. "But a minute more and those clothes would have been on the ground, and you know it."

Charged silence hummed between them.

"You don't own me," she warned quietly. "You don't have any say. Any right…"

"No? Well, maybe I want to," he answered.

Coop hadn't planned to say it just like that, but he hadn't planned on kissing her again, either. Kissing, hell. They'd been doing a foreplay dance and they both knew it. One taste of her and everything had exploded, just like the last time, only today she wasn't in such an emotionally fragile state.

And he'd admit to himself that he'd been a little edgy. He'd known since he'd opened the door and seen the uptight turn of her lips that she was going to say no. On the one hand he was relieved. Especially now, because he couldn't stop thinking about her. The truly crappy thing was that he actually agreed with her. They couldn't do this thing and go their separate ways. Not after today. He could hardly keep his hands off her.

Ironic, considering he'd been doing a great job of that for years now.

"You want to what?" she asked slowly, and he could hear the underlying threat.

"Have a right. Be important to you. Maybe I don't want to be the best friend who hears all your troubles. Maybe I don't want to be the guy who brings you a beer and makes you laugh, but doesn't get to go home with you at the end of the night. I've been doing that for years, Melissa, and I'm tired of it."

"What the…" She stepped back, her face white. "What are you saying, Coop? Years? Are you serious? Because I had the biggest crush on you when we were kids, and you were always so determined to stay friends. You weren't interested in me that way. We were buddies, remember?"

"Yeah, and I was an idiot. And by the time I realized it you'd had your cherry popped by my best friend."

She turned away as if slapped. He regretted his choice of words; they'd been harsh and indicative of his frustration. He closed his eyes and tried again. "I'm sorry, Mel. I shouldn't have put it that way."

"No," she said quietly, speaking to the water, "that was pretty clear and to the point."

"It's not your fault, okay? I'm frustrated. I didn't realize how I felt until you were with someone else. We were so young. I thought if I just waited it out, maybe I'd get another chance. And then you married him. What was I supposed to do?"

"You want me to feel bad for you?" She spread her arms wide. "I wasted years on that guy!"

"Why did you?" Coop asked. "I mean, no one forced you to marry him. People kept expecting you to break up. Most high school couples do, you know. So what did the great Scott have that made him such a prize?"

Her eyes blazed at him. "Don't even, Coop."

"Why? Because it's making you take a long hard look at your marriage? Was it his good looks? His charm? Money? What was it?"

"It was everything," she yelled. "It was everything, okay? He was there. He was in it and he asked. And you know what? I genuinely thought I loved him. It's not like I didn't care about him or he didn't care about me. Marrying him made sense, all right?"

"Except it was missing something."

"Yeah, well, we were trying to start a family, remember?"

Coop didn't know how she could be so blind. Did she really think her marriage had failed because of an infidelity? That was the easy and short answer, but he knew it was a lot more complicated than that. He knew more than he cared to, because he'd been caught right smack in the middle.

"I'm not talking about a family. I'm talking about love. I'm talking about soul mates. I'm talking about marrying the one person who gets you. The person people talk about when they say The One. And don't kid yourself. Scott knew he was somebody, but he also knew he wasn't The One."

"Don't be ridiculous."

But her eyes skittered away. He had hit on a nerve and he knew it.

"I'm sorry, Mel. I truly am."

She looked up. "He told you that?"

Coop nodded. "You've got to understand, I was friends with both of you. Guys don't unload like women, but sometimes things get said over a beer or two, especially when a man's troubled. He didn't know how to make you happy, and he could tell that you weren't. I told him he couldn't make you happy if he wasn't happy.

Then he laughed. And said that you'd married too young."

"We were twenty…"

Coop shoved his hands into his pockets. He wanted to reach out to her. She looked so forlorn, so alone. But it was time, wasn't it? Time she learned the whole truth.

"He knew you wanted a family, so he agreed to try, remember? I told him that kids wouldn't fix things. That was the first time he ever accused me of trying to push my own agenda. He said I didn't want you to have kids because that would complicate things when I made my move."

"Oh, Coop…" Her eyes widened. She came a little closer, hugging her arms around herself as if she was cold, even though the day was still mild. "Was it true?"

He swallowed against the pain that still managed to rear its head when he thought of those last six months before hell broke loose. "I would *never* have tried to break you up. But understand this, Mel—I knew you weren't happy, and it was killing me. We all still did things together, and we smiled and laughed a lot, and it was all churning around like acid in my stomach. And then I saw him one day, when I was on my way back from Edmonton. He was coming out of that motel—you know, the little one out by the highway? With her. At first I couldn't believe it was him, and that there must be a good explanation. And then he opened her car door and kissed her before she got in."

Silence followed his words. Not once had he shared the details of how he'd found out about Scott's affair. Coop had apologized, but until recently she'd never accepted his apology. He'd tried to explain and had always been cut short. He gave her time now to digest the truth.

She picked up a stone and tossed it into the creek. They both watched the splash and then it was gone.

"You asked him about it."

Her voice was hoarse and tired. He wondered how much more he should say, but then considered where they were and what they'd been doing, and knew he couldn't keep things hanging between them any longer. Not if they were going to move forward.

"I told him I saw him there. I expected him to deny it, but he didn't. He just shrugged and said, 'So what?' I told him that he had to put an end to it. And he asked why. Said that he was twenty-four years old, and did I really think he was going to sleep with the same woman for the rest of his life? When he said that, I lost it, Mel.

Things got heated. I said something about how he shouldn't have married you in the first place."

And Scott had been cunning and very astute. Coop could remember clearly the sneer on his friend's face as he turned into someone Coop didn't know. *That would clear the way for you,* Scott had said. *I see the way you look at her.* It had ripped his guts out, hearing that, because Scott was throwing away the one thing Coop would have given anything to have.

And his loyalty to Scott had died a very quick death.

He inhaled deeply, suddenly realizing he'd been silent for several seconds and that Mel was watching him curiously.

"Does it hurt to remember?" she asked quietly.

He nodded. "I demanded that he end it or I would tell you. And he laughed at me, Mel. He said that if I told you, he'd deny it. And he said you'd believe him, especially when he told you that I was in love with you and was making up stories to try to ruin your marriage."

She lifted her chin. "My God. And he thought I'd seriously believe him?"

"Wouldn't you? I'm pretty sure he could have given you a list of times I'd done or said something that was maybe a little too personal for a simple friend. At least enough to make you doubt. And let's face it. You would want to believe him because otherwise the truth meant…"

She heaved out a breath. "The truth would mean exactly what it meant in the end."

"I wanted to tell you so bad. As a friend, I owed that to you. But it was impossible, don't you see? All that would happen was that Scott would go on cheating, and you would hate me and we'd no longer be friends. I thought at least this way maybe you'd find out on your own, eventually, and…"

Her gaze was keen. "And you could be there to help me pick up the pieces?"

He hung his head. That sounded terrible. As if he was just waiting for his opportunity to move in. "Something like that," he admitted. "Please believe me, Mel, that my motives weren't opportunistic. I knew that you'd need a friend, someone to support you."

"Except when I found out, Scott told me that you already knew."

"He turned out to be not a very nice person when he was cornered," Coop said. "I couldn't be friends with him any longer. We had stopped hanging out.…"

"You'd started dating Sharla someone from Ponoka."

"Yeah." And before that it had been Christine, and Kirsten, and a bunch of others he hadn't cared for much, but who helped him pass the time. He always broke it off before things got heavy, or if he got the sense they were getting too close. He always tried the parting-as-friends thing before it got too intense.

"He hated you that much?"

Coop raised his shoulders and lowered them again. "He saw what you couldn't. That I cared for you too much. Add in the fact that he was well aware you were both unhappy…"

"And the past three years?"

The wind plus their kissing had taken her neat hairdo and shredded it. He thought it looked beautiful, all wispy around her face. He loved how she never shied away, but looked him dead in the eye, ready to face whatever was coming her way. She'd maybe been a little sweeter when she'd been a teenager, but Melissa was way stronger now, and he loved that about her.

"You told me you hated me. That you didn't want to speak to me ever again. It wasn't really the best time for me to tell you how I felt. Besides, you were right. I had let you down. I didn't like myself for what I'd done. For a while I was angry with you, too, for not seeing how I had been put in an impossible position. I stayed away because I had to find a way to let you go."

"Except here we are."

"Yes," he said, "here we are. Apparently that plan didn't work so well."

And he still loved her. He was as sure of that today as he'd been three, five, seven years ago. And he was equally sure that if he said so, she'd run back to Misty, jump in the saddle and be gone in the space of a heartbeat.

"I need to think about all of this." Mel unlocked her arms and pushed her hair back from her face. "It changes things."

"It doesn't, not really."

Her expression twisted with consternation. "Yeah, it does. Especially when you consider how…what we…" She frowned deeply. "This complicates everything, Coop. And more than ever, I'm positive that the last thing I should do is take you up on your offer. There's just too much history and too much drama. We could never be objective about it."

"I'm sorry, Mel. It seemed like a way to help you, that's all. To make up for all the crap that you've had to deal with. But you're right. I couldn't stand by and watch you carry my baby and stay on the sidelines. It's probably best."

It would also kill him to watch her carry

someone else's child, but he couldn't have it both ways. Unless by some miracle she gave up on the idea…

"Can we go back now, please? It's getting late. We're going to lose the light before much longer."

"Sure."

He needed to give her time. Time to digest all she'd learned and time to think about what had happened between them today. It was important. It wasn't going away. It would probably happen again. He knew it, and he was pretty sure she knew it, too.

He untied Sergeant while she put her foot in the stirrup and swung onto Misty's back. She didn't wait, but set off ahead of him, as familiar with the way back as he was.

There was history that she couldn't deny. There was something new she couldn't deny, either. And he knew how to be patient.

But not too patient. Not now that he'd had a taste of her and knew for sure what he'd always suspected. There were fireworks between them—on both sides. She could deny it for only so long. For the first time, he actually felt as if they might have a future.

And yet one question still nagged at the back of his mind. The one thing Mel wanted more than anything was a child. Were her feelings for him genuine, or were they a means to an end? The last thing he wanted was for Mel to be more in love with the idea of having his baby than with him. A relationship with that as its foundation would be doomed to failure, and there was too much at stake.

Once again, his heart was on the line. But this time he was prepared to risk it.

CHAPTER NINE

THE STRETCH OF WARM weather continued, making October feel more like early September. Mel worked in a T-shirt and her apron most days, finding long sleeves too warm. Amy came down with the flu that had been going around, and Melissa put in long, hard hours trying to keep up.

It was good to keep busy. After leaving Coop at the creek, she'd made good time getting back to the Double C barn, Coop and Sergeant following right behind. Bob had been at the barn already, talking to a man with a huge horse trailer and bigger truck. The rancher from Montana had arrived early, despite it being a holiday. Mel was saved from a long or awkward goodbye as Bob took care of Misty and Coop looked after business.

She was still trying to come to terms with everything she'd learned.

Coop had been in love with her when she was

married to Scott. Looking back now, perhaps there had been signs, but she'd been so caught up in herself and trying to make her marriage work that she'd missed them. She believed Coop now, though, when he said he'd wanted to tell her about Scott's indiscretion. It had been in the anguished tone of his voice, the way his eyes were wide and earnest as he explained.

But more troublesome than either of those things were the two truths she had to face.

One, Scott hadn't been the only party to blame in the failure of their marriage. Granted, he'd been utterly wrong to cheat. But they'd been in trouble for some time.

And two, Cooper Ford had the ability to make her feel as if she were going to fire off like a Roman candle.

She couldn't do a thing about the first now. But the second…what was she going to do about Coop?

She didn't have an answer for that, so she avoided him. Religiously. As long as he didn't venture into the flower shop, it was pretty safe. Right now it seemed as if all she did was work and sleep.

Her parents returned from their New England trip and invited her over for dinner. When questioned, she admitted she'd spent the holiday with the Ford family. Her mother and father were surprised and shared a significant look between them, but let the matter drop.

But after dinner, when her father had gone to watch his favorite game show, Mel and her mother were alone in the kitchen washing dishes. "So you and Cooper are on speaking terms," Roseanne said. "That's a surprise."

"It was time to let go of being mad. It doesn't matter anymore, right? Coop explained some of what was going on at the time. He was in a tough position. And honestly, Mom, my marriage wasn't what it should have been."

Rose set down the plate she was drying and put her hand on Mel's arm. "You've never admitted that before."

Melissa focused on the casserole dish she was scrubbing. "I didn't want to face how I'd messed up, too. It was easier to blame everyone else."

Rose withdrew her hand. "So you and Cooper…"

Mel shook her head. "Speaking terms. You said it yourself." She kept scrubbing. If Mel looked at her mother, Rose would see the lie.

"Hmm. I suppose this doesn't change your plans for…the other."

This was the problem. It had been so clear only a few weeks ago. She wanted a baby. She was going through steps to have a baby. Now she had to decide whether or not to try again, or try adopting, or… There shouldn't actually be another choice. She was still not interested in getting married. That hadn't changed. And yet she hadn't contacted the clinic, nor had she taken steps to sign up at the adoption registry.

"You're worried about what people will think," she said to Rose. "I get it. You know, I worried about that when it came to my marriage, and made sure all the outward appearances were beyond reproach. Inside we were a mess. I find I worry less about appearances these days, Mom."

Rose sighed. "I can deal with appearances. Honey, I worry about you. Being a parent isn't easy even at the best of times. I can't tell you how great it is to know that at the end of the day there's someone there. Just…there to share the load. So you're not alone."

Her words sent an ache through Mel. "To be honest, I've been too busy lately to worry about it much."

The conversation changed after that, but Mel knew very well that her mother would think it wonderful if she dropped the single-mom idea altogether. Later that night, lying in the dark, she told herself that she needed to refocus and get back to her plan. Maybe it wasn't ideal, but

Mel had learned ages ago that any situation was what a person made of it.

But when she closed her eyes, it was Coop she saw behind her eyelids. Coop, with his faded jeans and bedroom eyes and slightly crooked grin. Steady, reliable Coop, shaking a rancher's hand with a firm grip and a smile, wielding a hammer for a neighbor, stroking the mane of a fuzzy colt on a warm afternoon.

Coop.

The following Sunday Mel dressed in her favorite plum knit dress and black heeled boots and went to church, something she usually only did on special occasions and holidays, much to her mother's chagrin. She'd stopped going each week when the gossip about her divorce had reached a fever pitch, and she'd never gotten into the habit again. There was only so much she could face down with dignity. But today was special—the baptism of Callum and Avery's daughter, Nell. Melissa had been personally invited to the service and to lunch at the Shepard house afterward, and she couldn't say no.

She liked Avery. The pretty blonde had opened up her cupcake shop down the street and had fit into Cadence Creek society as if she'd always lived here. And Callum had come out of hiding, smiling and being a proud papa. When they'd stopped in at the shop asking if she'd do a few special arrangements for the church, she'd agreed without a moment's hesitation.

The church was packed. She spotted her parents halfway up on the left, but their pew was full. She waggled her fingers at them and scanned the sanctuary for a free space. A pair of fingers waggled back at her—Jean Ford. Was there really nowhere else to sit? But Mel didn't see any sign of Coop, so it was probably safe. She walked up the aisle and slid into the seat. "Thanks," she said to Jean. "It's full up today."

"Baptisms usually are," Jean remarked. "And everyone is so taken with Callum and Avery and that little Nell. She's such a doll. Callum's family even came up from the lower mainland."

Mel stretched her neck to peer at the front of the church. Sure enough, in the front pew with Callum and Avery was another couple—Callum's parents, she guessed—and a younger man and woman, who each bore a striking resemblance to Callum. "Brother and sister?"

"Yes. Apparently she's some big event planner in Vancouver and is going to help Avery with the wedding. They're getting married at Christmas, you know."

"I hadn't heard. Last I spoke to Callum, he was buying flowers and an engagement ring."

"Fancy meeting you here."

Tingles shivered up her spine as a warm hip nudged against hers on her left. Everyone scooched over a bit, but it was still rather cozy when Cooper slid in beside her.

"I didn't think you were coming," Melissa whispered.

"Or you would have sat somewhere else?"

"Something like that."

He chuckled, the sound low and intimate. "It's church. I think you're pretty safe."

Except that this was a small town and they were two people of the same age sitting together at a church service. That was tantamount to an announcement.

The service started and Cooper of course hadn't grabbed a bulletin, so Mel was forced to share hers as they went through the opening prayers and announcements. They stood up to sing the first hymn and she was ultra-aware of him. He'd left off the jeans today and wore dress pants and shoes along with a striped shirt and tie. And he smelled good—as if he'd just gotten out of the shower and dashed on some über-masculine cologne loaded with pheromones or something. He sang on key but quietly, and once, when she turned the page of the hymnbook, he slid his finger over to brace the spine, and his skin brushed against hers.

This was church. There should not be butterflies winging their way through her stomach at a simple touch of finger to wrist. Or, as they sat down, at the pressure of his hip pressed against hers.

She definitely should be listening to the scripture rather than remembering being kissed beside the creek.

Coop was a mighty distraction through most of the service, but after the sermon came the baptism. Callum and Avery rose and went to the front, Nell cradled in Avery's arms, dressed in a flowing white christening gown. A lump formed in Mel's throat as she watched the proceedings. Callum's hand was along the small of Avery's back and they were both smiling. The minister reached for Nell and went through the ritual, saying the words and making the sign of the cross on her forehead with the water. It was so beautiful, watching them as a family. This was what Mel wanted so badly. They looked so close, like a real unit up there. She knew she could still go through with it all and do it alone, but she finally acknowledged that a small part of her longed for the total package: husband, wife, family.

And that scared her to death.

Nell started to fuss and the minister handed her over to Callum. The baby looked so small and fragile and white in Callum's big, broad arms. She cried for a moment, but Callum nestled her in the crook of his elbow and she settled.

Coop reached over and, between their thighs, cupped Melissa's hand in his.

That one, innocent touch took her reinforced, guarded heart and put a crack right down the center of it.

He squeezed her fingers as the baptism ended, and she squeezed back. He knew. He understood. More than anyone else had or would, he knew what she was feeling in this moment.

When she had been fourteen, Coop had been the guy who had just *got* her. Even if they'd argued, there'd been no drama as there was with girlfriends. The next day it was like nothing had happened. It had been so easy with him. The only thing she'd wanted was for him to look at her like she was a girl.

He was surely looking at her that way now. But she wasn't the same girl she'd been. Back then she'd had an open heart. He could have had it for the asking. Now she didn't trust so easily.

She hoped nobody could see them holding hands, but she didn't pull out of his grasp. It felt too good. Like an anchor in a day that would otherwise make her think and feel a little too much about all that was missing from her life.

He released her fingers when the last hymn was announced, sharing the hymnbook once more and putting it away during the benediction.

When everyone filtered out of the church, Mel took care to slide over next to her parents and walk out with them rather than remain paired up with Cooper. But outside they went their separate ways; Melissa had brought her own car in anticipation of driving out to Callum's, and her parents hadn't been invited to the lunch. Likewise, Bob and Jean left while Coop remained in the middle of the throng in the sunshine, talking and laughing with Ty and Sam Diamond while their wives, Clara and Angela, buttoned their kids' jackets.

Coop caught Mel's eye, and without breaking the link, put a hand on Sam's arm and excused himself.

She really, really wished he wasn't so good-looking. Wished that she could stop thinking of him in more-than-friendly ways. Wished they had less history, less baggage, so she could explore the attraction burning between them. But of anyone in this town, Cooper was the one man with whom she could not play games. He was too important.

"Hey," he said, coming to stand in front of her. "I didn't have a chance to say it before, but you look pretty today."

"Thanks." She chanced a look into his eyes and her whole body seemed to warm beneath the appraising glow.

"You going out to the lunch? I hear Martha Bullock is putting on the spread."

Martha was the best cook in Cadence Creek and the owner of the Wagon Wheel diner, not to mention the mother of their friend Rhys. "I was invited, yes."

"Want to drive out there together?"

Mel scanned the parking lot, and there was no denying that at least some members of the throng were curious. "I don't think so, but thanks. I'll take my own car."

"Screw gossip," he said easily.

Her gaze flickered to his and she kept a smile pasted on. "Easy for you to say."

A shadow passed over his face, just a little one, but she noticed it. Lately she seemed to notice everything. "It was really bad, wasn't it?" he asked.

"Yes. The worst was the pity. Poor Melissa,

hadn't had a clue what was going on right under her nose. But I don't like being the topic of the week under any circumstances. I'll see you out there, okay?"

"Fair enough."

But before he left, he gave her arm a squeeze. She felt the heat of it through the knitted sleeve and bit down on her lip. Cooper wasn't giving up. And knowing what she did now about his feelings and how deep they went, she felt a strange pressure to equal his devotion or just let him go. The worst thing was, she didn't quite know how to do either.

He was just going to have to be patient, she thought as she got into her car. He'd have to wait until she thought things through.

Cars and trucks lined one side of Callum's gravel driveway, parked on the grass. The beautiful fall weather meant that the party was set up outside. People brought their own lawn chairs, but the food was organized on tables beneath a collapsible gazebo. Mel opened the trunk and took out her foldable chair, and then made her way to where people were gathered. After depositing her chair, she went to offer her congratulations to Callum and Avery.

"Thanks for inviting me," she said, giving Avery a quick hug. "It was a beautiful service."

"The flowers were so pretty," Avery declared. "You'll do the ones for our wedding, won't you?"

Mel's heart warmed. "Of course I will. And look at this christening gown." Callum still held Nell in his arms and Mel touched the lace edge of the hem. "Where did you ever find it?"

Callum smiled. "My mom and dad bought it. The one they used for us was too small. Nell's six months old now."

Avery touched Callum's arm. "Be right back, okay?" She scooted off to greet the minister and his wife as they arrived.

"She's precious," Mel said. "And looks just like you, Callum."

"Poor girl. Would you hold her for a moment? I'm going to grab a few extra chairs. I don't think the minister brought any."

"Sure."

What else could she say? Mel's heart thrummed heavily as she reached out and took the baby in her arms. The satin-and-lace dress was silky against her skin and Nell smelled like baby lotion. "Hello there," Melissa said quietly, unable to stop the smile from spreading across her face. "Look at you, gorgeous girl."

Blue eyes stared up at her from beneath long,

dark lashes, and Mel pressed a kiss to the soft, fine hair. "Oh my," she whispered, and by simple instinct rocked her hips back and forth a little. To her surprise, Nell, who'd been the center of attention for quite a while, tucked her head into the curve of Mel's neck. Mel felt a tiny wet spot of baby drool just above the collar of her dress. It was a wonderful feeling. She'd be a good mother, she just knew it. And then her little house wouldn't seem quite so lonely.

She turned around and found Cooper watching them.

Her heart squeezed. He was standing with Rhys Bullock, but his gaze was locked on her and his dark eyes fairly glowed with what looked like appreciation and possession.

"Excuse me, you're Melissa, right?"

Mel broke her gaze away from Coop and turned to the voice on her left. The woman wasn't from Cadence Creek. While Mel had felt quite dressed up in her dress and boots, this woman made her feel slightly dowdy. It wasn't that she was heart-stoppingly gorgeous, not in the strictest sense of the word. But she had an aura of worldliness and capability that Mel envied—and all that from a simple greeting.

"Yes, I'm Melissa."

The woman held out her hand and smiled. "Hi. I'm Taylor Shepard, Callum's sister."

"The one from Vancouver. The event planner."

"That's me."

The woman practically oozed sophistication. Her dress was simply cut and color blocked with red, black and tan, and her designer shoes were black but with impossibly high heels showcasing perfect legs. Her dark hair was pulled back and braided on an angle so the tail fell over one shoulder.

Mel shook Taylor's hand quickly, then shifted Nell's weight on her arm. Taylor smiled. "She's something, isn't she? I still can't believe my big brother's a dad."

That statement helped make Mel feel slightly less inadequate. "She really is," Mel replied. "Callum's a completely different person since the two of them came into his life."

"Oh, he's not, not really. He's just back to the man we all knew and loved. Anyway, I'm going to be around a bit, helping Avery plan the wedding. Sort of my wedding gift to them. She told me you did the flowers for today and I wanted to touch base and introduce myself. I'm sure we're going to be seeing more of each other."

"And your other brother's here, too, right?"

"Yeah, Jack's here for another few days. Said he wants to explore the area. He's the sporty one in our family, so all this open space and proximity to the mountains has him pretty jazzed. Speaking of, I'd better get back. I told Martha Bullock that I'd help and I'm over here socializing instead. Nice to meet you, Melissa."

"Just call me Mel. Everyone else does."

Taylor smiled, stroked Nell's cheek lightly. "You've got the touch," she said softly. "She's asleep."

Melissa angled her head to look down at the baby as Taylor walked away, perfectly balanced on her stilettos. She was right. Nell had drifted off, completely relaxed in Mel's arms.

"Looks good on you," Coop said, from just behind her. His voice was soft and low and sent shivers down her spine.

"You have to stop sneaking up on me," she replied. She kept one hand on Nell's back, lightly rubbing.

"I do?"

"Coop."

She said it with such meaning that he laughed.

She sighed. "I thought after the other day…"

"That I'd give up?" He shook his head. "You needed time to think. I got that. I backed off. I didn't go away."

"I sort of wish you would."

"You don't mean that."

She wished she did. She wanted to mean it. It would make things so much simpler.

"You are seriously messing with my plans," she murmured. "It was easier when I was mad at you and not…"

She didn't finish the sentence, but Coop did it for her. "Not thinking about kissing me all the time?"

"I'm not thinking that!" She said it a little louder, and Nell shifted in her arms. "I'm not," she said quietly, frowning at him.

"You are such a liar," he replied easily.

"Coop…"

"See? You can't even come up with a good argument other than I'm messing around with your plans. Why does everything have to be planned out, anyway?"

"Less chance of disappointment," she answered promptly.

"Ah, says the voice of the disappointed," he replied.

The truth stung a bit and she lifted her chin.

"Oh, now don't get all like that," he cautioned. "I know I dumped a lot of information on you the other day and I know you've had a lot to think about. But you think too much. The truth of it is, you had a crush on me when I was too stupid to realize it, and I had a thing for you when you weren't available. Now we're both here and we're both available and all I'm suggesting is that we see where things go. Nothing heavy."

"Things are heavy with you by definition, Cooper. Because of our history."

"Forget history," he replied, coming a step closer. "I'm tired of the past getting in my way, aren't you? Let's forget about Scott and everything else and just focus on the present."

It sounded so tempting. "I know I've let him influence my life far too much." She had. She told herself and everyone else that he had no effect on her life, but that wasn't true. His affair and their divorce had changed everything, and colored every part of her life even now. She didn't like it, but she'd learned lessons that she didn't ever want to forget.

"You have a chance to start over," Coop said, his voice persuasive. "Go out on a date with me."

"A date?"

"You do remember what those are, right? I pick you up and we go somewhere like dinner or a movie. Then I drive you home."

"You're seriously asking me out on a date?"

"Yes. A real date. Not meeting up at some

town get-together or hanging out at my parents' place."

She shouldn't say yes. Coop was so complicated, but the idea of truly shedding the past and having an actual date sounded heavenly. When had she last done that? When she was about nineteen. Then she'd been married, and date night wasn't quite the same. Then even those had stopped—and there'd been none since. Good Lord. She was twenty-seven and she hadn't been on a date in years.

"Where would we go?"

He grinned. "You let me take care of that. You're saying yes?"

"I'm saying yes. To one date."

"I'll pick you up Saturday night at seven. That gives you enough time to get ready after closing, right?"

She nodded, excitement building in her chest. She was going out and didn't know where. What should she wear?

Neither of them noticed Avery approach until she spoke. "Mel, your arms must be ready to fall off. Thanks for watching Nell for so long. Callum went for chairs and I got sidetracked…"

"It was no trouble." She shifted her arms and slid the sleeping baby into her mother's embrace.

"Oh, she's left a drool spot on your dress," Avery said apologetically.

Mel looked down at the damp circle and gave a soft smile. "Don't worry," she answered. "I love babies. It was a real treat to have her so relaxed. Besides, this gets tossed right in the washing machine."

"Well, you two should get some food. Martha's put on a great spread."

"Thanks."

When she was gone, the silence got a little awkward. "Listen," Coop said, "I'm going to talk to Ty about a mare he's just bought, but I'll see you Saturday, right?"

"Saturday," she echoed.

He smiled, then let his gaze drift down her body. "Oh, and Mel?" He winked before he turned away. "Wear those boots."

She watched him walk off, admiring the view. After thinking of him as a friend for so long, and then as an enemy, it was quite shocking to realize that she was now thinking about him in a totally different manner altogether. One that made her temperature rise considerably.

He wanted to put the past behind them, forget it existed. That sounded good in theory, but there was just one problem. It was impossible, because the past gave them context. And it was impossible because he was making her feel fifteen again, young and nervous and craving a kiss from him. Just like then, she thought about him *all the time*. And that didn't fit anywhere in her formerly well-ordered plans.

CHAPTER TEN

SHE IGNORED THE ORDER to wear the boots. Instead Mel went shopping. The first "first date" in years deserved a new outfit, and she rarely spent money on herself anymore. Wednesday, after the store closed for the day, she drove to the West Edmonton Mall, determined to find something new and pretty. She liked the result as she stood in front of her bedroom mirror. The black pencil skirt hugged her hips like a dream, and the ivory blouse with its black collar and cuffs made her feel feminine and pretty. Best of all, though, were the shoes. The heels were higher than she normally wore, but manageable due to the platforms in the toe, and they did magical things for her calves.

He would be here at any moment....

Her doorbell rang and she jumped, stared at her wide eyes and pressed a finger to her freshly lipsticked lips. He was here. Coop. As a date. A new beginning for both of them.

Her heels clattered as she crossed the hardwood floor to the front door. Taking a breath and hoping she wasn't blushing, she opened it.

Coop was on the step and he held out a bouquet of flowers. "I know it's weird giving a florist flowers, but…"

He'd brought her three roses, red ones, wrapped up with baby's breath. She didn't even care if they were a cliché and from the grocery store—it was too special. "Not at all," she said, hoping he didn't hear the nervous tremor in her voice. "Come on in while I put these in some water."

He waited just inside the door as she escaped to the kitchen, her heart hammering against her ribs. When she returned she nearly swallowed her tongue, he looked so delicious. Once again he'd left the cowboy hat at home, but he'd kept the jeans—dressier ones—with spit-shined boots, a white shirt with the top button undone and a caramel-colored sport coat.

"You look amazing," he said, pushing the panels of his coat back and hooking his thumbs in his pockets. "Really…amazing."

"I went shopping," she explained, belatedly realizing he'd know she went especially for tonight. She hid her face inside the closet as she reached for her coat.

He took it from her and helped her put it on.

When he smoothed it over her shoulders, his hands paused. He was standing close behind her, the air between them filled with silent possibility. "We'd better go," he said roughly. "Or we're not going to get there at all."

Funny how one little sentence could nearly send her into complete meltdown. She prayed her knees would hold out as she reached for her purse and stepped away from the warmth of his body. Coop moved aside and held open the door, letting her out into the cool autumn air.

It helped, getting outside. Coop caught up to her at the bottom of the steps. "I borrowed Mom's car. I thought it might be nicer than going in a huge pickup."

Once more he held the door for Mel, closing it behind her when she'd slid into the car.

During the drive into the city Coop thankfully kept the conversation neutral, chatting about town events and what was going on at the Double C. But the whole time Mel was thinking about what would happen when he drove her home; not if he would walk her to the door, but if she would ask him in.

Coop tried to talk about every possible subject during the drive to the restaurant. Anything to distract him from the way Mel looked tonight.

She'd dressed up. For him. The tidy little skirt illuminated every curve, and the blouse she was wearing made her look a little like a librarian fantasy. All she was missing was the glasses. And he was glad she hadn't taken his suggestion of the heeled boots, because seeing her in those shoes…

His first impulse was to not even leave her house.

But he'd promised a first date, and a first date she was going to get. So he'd held her coat and the door, and tried to think of other things besides getting her out of that killer outfit piece by piece.

They had reservations at an Italian place in downtown Edmonton. Once they were seated, they each ordered a glass of wine and scanned the menu. He was nervous. He was with a woman he'd known most of his life and he was suddenly unsure of what to say or do. When their drinks came and they'd ordered, it was Mel who held up her glass and offered a toast. "To starting over," she said.

"To new beginnings," he echoed, clinking the rim to hers. He watched her lips touch the glass as she drank, and he took a bigger gulp than he intended.

They kept the conversation neutral as they dug

into their antipasti and then main courses—he had a spicy pappardelle and Mel had a truffle ravioli that looked delicious, along with a second glass of wine. She made him laugh as she told him about how someone's dog had got loose, run in the store, investigated every corner and then, to everyone's horror, lifted his leg on Amy's expensive handbag—clearly not as funny for Amy as it was for Mel. He talked to her about his plans for the ranch, the new stud stallion he was buying and how he was asked to speak at a conference coming up in Colorado. It was the strangest, best first date he'd ever had—getting to know someone he'd known all his life. New and yet familiar. And exciting. Oh yes, exciting. He didn't want the evening to end, but he couldn't wait, either.

They lingered over dessert, ordering coffee and a rich chocolate *torta* laced with hazelnuts. Somehow they ended up missing a spoon, and Mel had used hers to add cream to her coffee. Coop spooned up a little of the *torta* and held it out for her to taste.

"Coop…" she chided, raising one eyebrow. But he saw the longing in her eyes and waited, holding her gaze. Watching it heat as the moment drew out.

She leaned forward and took the dessert from

the spoon. Closed her eyes and sighed. "Oh, that's good."

He wasn't sure how he was going to be able to drive the forty minutes back to her house.

He tasted the chocolate confection and agreed it was delicious. But he derived far more enjoyment from feeding it to her from the spoon. The fact that she accepted it without argument took things a step further with them tonight. This was going somewhere. Where, he wasn't exactly sure. But he was looking forward to finding out.

The drive back to Cadence Creek was quiet, the car filled with delicious tension. He reached over once and held her hand, driving with his left. Her fingers twined with his and she looked at him and smiled lazily. "Sorry I'm not such a good conversationalist," she said, leaning her head back on the seat. "A long day, full stomach and two glasses of wine have made me sleepy."

Disappointment threaded through him, but he smiled back anyway. "It was a good night."

"As first dates go, it was top-notch."

He hit the exit for Cadence Creek and started down the secondary highway that led to town.

It was after ten o'clock and Mel's quiet street was mostly dark, save a few lights over front doors. "Not much happening here on a Saturday night," Coop commented, pulling into her driveway.

"You know how it is," she said with a smile. "If you want to get into some trouble, you do it outside town limits."

He was thinking he could get into a fair bit of trouble inside town limits without much effort. "Hang on," he commanded, and got out of the car, jogged around the front and opened her door.

She pivoted and put her legs out first before reaching for the door frame and boosting herself up.

"Mel, if I can just say one thing…damn, you've got the greatest legs."

She blushed. Even in the dim glow of her porch light he could see the color touch her cheeks. He shut the door and walked her to the steps, but before she could put her foot on the first one he grabbed her hand and pulled her back.

"I want to do this and I don't want to do it in the light," he whispered, and then he finally—finally—kissed her.

He took his time. He wasn't some callow teenager in a hormonal hurry to get to the end zone. He pulled her close, twined his fingers into her hair and explored her mouth as if he had all the time in the world.

Just like before, passion exploded between them. It was thrilling, knowing that it wasn't just an emotionally heightened situation causing things to run hot, but actual chemistry. Her heels put her eyes on a level with his nose, so that he had to tip her head only the slightest bit to have full access to her mouth. He fumbled with the large buttons on her wool coat, opening it and slipping his arms inside, pulling her flush against his body.

"Mmm," she said into his mouth, a little impatient sound as she pushed away. But she only did it to spread his sport coat wide as well, so that they were pressed together, cotton shirt to flimsy blouse, with all their body heat between them.

Kissing was all well and good, but eventually it did have to lead somewhere, and right now all Cooper could think of was making love to her. "Invite me inside," he said against her lips.

She didn't answer, just ran her fingers through his hair, pulling his head down so she could kiss him again. What else could he do but oblige?

But after a few minutes more, with their breathing heavier and his hands roaming farther than he'd planned—especially while still in her front yard—he put his palm along the side of her face and forced her to look at him. "Invite me in," he commanded again.

"I…I can't," she stuttered, her breath coming in short gasps.

"Sure you can," he replied smoothly. "You say, Coop, would you like to come inside?"

She shook her head. "If we go inside, we're going to…you're going to…"

"With any luck," he answered. And he'd thought ahead. Inside his coat pocket was a condom. For a second he paused, wondering how she'd react to the insistence for birth control. But he had to know she was with him for him, and not for his genetic material.

He pushed the thought away. Mel wouldn't do such a thing; he knew her better than that. And he wanted her more than he could remember ever wanting a woman before. To help convince her, he ran his hand beneath the flap of her coat, down her shoulder and over one tightly peaked breast. She shuddered.

"Coop?"

"Yes, honey?"

She grabbed his wrists and stepped back a little. "I am not the kind of girl who puts out on the first date."

Dammit. "Are you sure?"

"I'm very, very sure." She blinked at him. She meant it, the sassy thing. And he'd better get control of himself in a hurry if he had any hope of leaving this situation gracefully. And possibly making her regret her decision. Because if they kept on this way, it was going to happen sooner or later. Given how he was feeling right now, he prayed it was sooner.

"You realize you're killing me here."

She nodded slowly.

He sighed. "Damn you, Melissa, for making me behave."

She laughed at him. "You know the show biz motto, Always Leave Them Wanting More?"

He couldn't help it; she looked so impish and sexy and wonderful that he chuckled. It might be killing him, but he'd wait. It would be worth it.

He was in love with her. Any doubts about that had fled at Thanksgiving. How she'd held his hand at the baptism, the date tonight—it all told him he had a chance if he played his cards right. At this moment that meant stepping back and giving her time.

"Okay." He gave in, releasing her completely. "You win."

"Thank you for a wonderful evening, though."

He put his hand in his pocket. "You up for a second date?"

"Even though I'm sending you away...unsatisfied?"

"I thought you said you were leaving me wanting more. I want more."

The air sizzled between them. "We're going to do this, then?" she asked quietly.

"I want to. I want to see where it leads. Don't you? It doesn't have to be any heavier than that. Let's just see where it takes us, Mel."

"And what if it doesn't work?"

The smile slid from his face as the tone suddenly turned serious. "Then we can say we tried. And no matter what, we stay friends. No more going back to the way things were, I promise."

"I promise, too. I didn't really enjoy hating you all that much."

"When can I see you again?" He didn't want to wait a week. Or even days. He wanted to see her as often as he could. Every minute.

"I suppose Tuesday-night bingo at the community center doesn't float your boat."

"I could live through it if you were there."

She laughed then, a light, musical laugh that he hadn't heard in years. "I won't make you do that," she replied. "Let's just meet up for dinner at the diner, then go for a walk or something."

It sounded perfectly boring. "If that's what you want."

"I'll meet you there at six, right after the store closes. How does that sound?"

He'd rather she asked him here for a private dinner for two, but she was bent on taking it slow. His head told him that was the right move, no matter what his libido was screaming right now.

"Perfect."

"Coop?"

"Hmm?"

"Kiss me once more before you go?"

Kissing her was the easy part of the request. The just once part? He was going to have trouble with that.

For two weeks Mel let herself be wooed into Coop's definition of dating. They went to the diner on Tuesday and decided on burgers and fries and milkshakes as a throwback to high school days, then took a long walk along the creek in the dark. He stopped by the shop once with a bag lunch and convinced her to eat with him on a bench along Main Street, soaking up the sun. On Saturday they drove to Edmonton for a movie, sat near the back of the theater and held hands. The next week they took a short drive to the coffee shop out on the highway for dessert, and she took a precious few hours one afternoon to go riding out at the Double C.

There were kisses, but Coop was on his best behavior, with no more suggestions to take things further. Which was a shame, because being kissed at the door was leaving her distinctly unsatisfied. If he was trying to leave *her* wanting more, he was definitely succeeding.

They made plans to eat at the diner again, and Melissa told herself that tonight she was going to ask him to her place for their next date. She could cook and they could share a meal without being so incredibly visible to the town. Besides, she had a very nice sofa in her living room and she wouldn't mind more than a few stolen kisses outside the circle of her porch light.

She dressed for their date when she went to work, as she'd head to the Wagon Wheel as soon as she turned over the Closed sign. Mel wore the boots he'd admired that Sunday at Callum's. She chose them because he liked them, and it meant she could wear one of her favorite outfits—snug denim leggings and a scoop-neck tee with her sweater-coat overtop. It was casual but fun, and she put her hair up. Maybe when Coop walked her home, he'd take the clip out and run his hands through her hair the way he seemed to enjoy....

Tuesdays weren't the busiest night at the Wagon Wheel, and when she walked in the atmosphere was relaxed and friendly. A few tables were occupied, a gray-haired man was putting quarters into the genuine jukebox, and the twang of a country classic filled the air. Off to one side she saw Coop. He was early and was talking to Clara and Ty Diamond. Melissa took a minute to simply stare at him and appreciate the scenery. Mercy, he was good-looking. No one could wear a pair of jeans like Coop. The denim was wearing around the pockets, the faded spots strategically placed for her viewing pleasure.

Beside him, Clara was in maternity clothing, and as she was reaching into a diaper bag, her one-year-old daughter, Susanna, made a wobbly dash down the aisle between booths. With a laugh Coop reached out and snagged her midstride, scooping her into his arms.

Instead of fussing or squirming, the little girl giggled, reached out and patted his face. He said something and then tapped his cheek with his finger. Susanna leaned forward and delivered one sloppy wet baby kiss there. Mel was dangerously close to melting. Then Coop's eyes closed—just for a second—and he gave the baby a tender kiss on the head before handing her to her father.

It was a strange moment for Mel to realize that she was in love with him. Not just sentimentally affected, or that she *could* love him, but that she *did*—a bone-deep, right-to-the-center-of-her-soul kind of love. So much for taking it slow and seeing where it went. Or being in any way casual about what was happening between them.

She loved him. She loved him so much that it was freaking her out right now. So much that it was suddenly hard to breathe and she could feel the beginnings of an anxiety attack. This wasn't supposed to happen. They were supposed to be casually dating. Exploring. Not… Oh God. Not this. She couldn't do *this*.

She slipped out the door before he could see that she'd arrived and jogged away from the diner, trying to put some distance between them. Her breath came in shallow gasps. When she turned the corner, she stopped and pressed her hand to her chest, trying to steady her breathing. He was going to be expecting her at any moment, but she couldn't go back there. Couldn't go in and have supper and act as if everything was all right. It wasn't. She didn't know what to do with the sudden rush of feeling.

For the longest time she hadn't been sure she was even capable of being in love. She'd thought she was before, but recognized now that she'd been far more enamored with the idea of love than actually in it up to her eyeballs. But here it was, and it honestly felt as if the earth had fallen away beneath her feet.

She pulled her cell phone from her purse and sent him a quick text message, saying she wasn't feeling well and needed to take a rain check, and that she'd call him later.

Once at home she changed into fleecy pajamas and shoved her hair into a ponytail. What was she going to do? She wasn't ready for this, and she certainly wasn't ready to tell Coop how she felt. She was smart enough to know that the reason she'd been so very angry with Coop all this time was because she'd felt betrayed and abandoned, and it had damn near killed her. It had been the darkest period in her life—realizing that her husband didn't love her, and losing her best friend. She'd understood then that she was an easy woman to leave. And she'd promised never to let herself be that emotionally vulnerable again.

And here she was. She'd let down her guard, agreed to make amends, and found herself in a worse predicament than she could ever imagine. She loved him. Something he'd said that day at the creek echoed in her head: *I'm not sure you ever get over someone you really love.* It was time she faced the worst truth of all. The greatest loss from the breakup of her marriage wasn't her husband, but her best friend. *He* was the one she couldn't get over. And if they took this thing all the way and it didn't work out…

It would be ten times worse. A hundred. She would be…empty.

She reached for the tissues. This had truly gone beyond taking it easy and enjoying each other's company, beyond seeing where it would lead. This was the real deal. She knew, because it had never hurt to love this way before. It had never caused this paralyzing fear.

The third tissue was balled up and thrown on the floor when there was a knock on her door. She knew without asking that it was Coop. She should have known that a text message wouldn't keep him away.

"Mel? Open up."

She wiped her eyes and went to the door, knowing he'd knock until she opened it. Hopefully, she didn't look too bad; at least with the runny nose she might be able to fake it. There was no way she was going to let on the real reason she had red eyes and was in her pj's. She had to sort through her feelings before she could have this conversation with Coop.

"Just a sec," she called, deliberately making her voice sound stuffy. She took a deep breath and opened the door.

"Dear God, you look awful."

He, on the other hand, looked amazing. He always did. The jean jacket was back and so was the plaid shirt, only it was clean for their "date." His hat was perched on his head, throwing his face half in shadow. It was dead sexy, and she felt her resolve weaken.

"I don't know if it's allergies or a fall cold, but my head is plugged," she lied.

"Allergies? But you're a florist."

Damn. She was so off her game. She forced a shrug. "Fall cold then. Sorry, Coop."

He bent his knees a bit so that he was on eye level with her. She stayed still beneath his scrutiny.

Coop rose up again and held out a paper bag. "Martha put together a container of chicken soup for you."

Her throat clogged again. Of course. She'd said she wasn't feeling well and Coop had decided to make her feel better. As if she needed one more reason to love him.

"That's so sweet." She reached out and took the bag.

"You sure you're okay? Do you need anything?" A wrinkle formed between his eyebrows.

She hated lying. She was certain he could see right through it. But how could she possibly come right out and say what was going on? Considering what he'd told her about his own feelings, she wasn't ready to be that open. That honest. That…intense. That was it. Things would get really intense, and right now just realizing that she even had these feelings was overwhelming. She needed time. Time to decide what to do. What she wanted. Time to simply get used to the idea.

Not just that. She was in love with her best friend. Perhaps they'd taken a hiatus, but she knew deep down that was what Coop was. He'd been her best friend, and the last two weeks had shown her how close they still could be. There was something so very heavy about having this many feelings for one person. So much potential for things to go wrong.

So much to lose.

"I'm going to be fine, really," she assured him. "I'm going to eat my soup and go to bed, and I know I'll be much better tomorrow."

He looked disappointed that she didn't ask him in, just stood in the doorway to her house, shutting him out. "If you're sure…"

"I am. But thank you, Coop. For the soup. And sorry about tonight."

"It's no biggie. We'll do it another time." He stepped ahead and planted a gentle kiss on her forehead. "Feel better."

He went back to his truck and she shut the door.

What on earth was she going to do now? She couldn't avoid him forever. Nor did she want to.

She just needed time to think. To sort things out. And to make a plan.

CHAPTER ELEVEN

COOP KNEW DAMNED well that whatever had made Mel's eyes puffy and red, it was no allergic reaction or fall cold. That kind of look only came from hard crying. She could sound as congested as she wanted, but he knew. She'd blown off their date and she'd been home crying, and whatever had gotten her upset, she'd been so determined to keep it from him that she'd lied about it. The last time she'd had a hard cry, she'd gotten her period. Though he hated it, a little voice inside him asked what else she might have lied about. They'd never talked about her giving up her plans for IUI. He'd just assumed, when they started seeing each other…

He watched one of the hands bring a dun-colored stallion named Crapshoot back to the stable. Standing at over sixteen hands, he was a big, beautifully muscled animal whose strong hindquarters could turn on a dime. He'd bring a pretty penny, but Coop was tempted to keep him for himself.

Tonight, though, he wasn't in the mood to spend longer in the stables. He was restless. It was clear to him that Mel was avoiding his calls, and in the ones she did take she said things like it was really busy at the store, or she was on her way out the door. It annoyed the hell out of him. Almost as much as it hurt. He hadn't expected her to blow him off. Not like this.

Then again, he always did make a habit of expecting more from Mel than she delivered.

A small voice inside told him that wasn't fair, but he was mad enough that he didn't listen. Not just mad. Afraid. Being with her these last few weeks had taken all the feelings he'd tamped down and given them the opportunity to run free. He'd stopped imagining what it would be like to hold her in his arms because she'd actually been there. He knew what she tasted like, the way she melted against him, the sound of her voice on the phone late at night. He'd given himself permission to love her again. And boy, did it hurt.

Enough was enough. If this wasn't going to work, he had to know. Playing games, not being honest—they couldn't maintain a friendship that way. And even though the very idea tasted like ashes in his mouth, he knew that was what he'd promised. Friendship.

It was full-on dark by the time he'd showered and got up the gumption to drive over to her house. Light glowed from the front window—her living room—and it flickered, letting him know she had the television on. A week ago they would have been out together, having coffee or looking at the stars or just talking on the phone. Not now. Something drastic had changed, and he wanted to know what.

He knocked on the door.

It took a minute, but finally the dead bolt clicked back and she opened it. "Hey," she said.

"You look like you're feeling better."

She smiled softly and it damn near broke his heart. "I am, thank you."

"Can I come in, Mel?"

His gaze caught hers. Her eyes were wide and soft and he lost himself there for a moment. Then she lowered her lashes and stepped back. "Of course. Come on in. I'm just switching some laundry over, but I'll be right back. Make yourself at home."

The television was turned on to a popular crime drama and there was a cup of tea, half-gone, on the end table next to the sofa. He took off his hat and put it on the back of a chair, then ambled through to her kitchen. It was cozy and warm, painted a soft cream with dark red accents. The oak table had a red plaid place mat in the middle and there was a small bouquet of flowers, too.

It was strange that he'd never seen her kitchen before, but she'd always made sure they went somewhere else on their dates. The closest he'd ever come to inside was helping her with her coat the night they'd first gone to dinner.

By keeping him out of her house she was always able to keep him at arm's length. Never let him too close. He got it now, and felt just a little bit like a fool.

He heard the beep of the washing machine somewhere in the hall behind the garage. Absently, he picked up a stack of adverts from the mail that was strewn on the counter, flipping through flyers and coupons. A slip of paper fell to the floor. He picked it up and saw the scribbled appointment in Mel's delicate handwriting. The appointment had been for two days ago. His heart tumbled down to his toes. He should have listened to the warnings in his head.

She came back from the laundry room and stopped short at the sight of him in the kitchen. "Oh," she said, then gave a small smile. "Can I get you something to drink, Coop? I was having tea, but I've got other stuff in the…"

"Cut the small talk, Mel. I don't have the stomach for it."

Her eyes widened and her cheeks paled at his sharp tone. "Okay, let's cut to the chase then. Why are you here?"

"To find out why you've suddenly started blowing me off. Looks like your cold is all better, by the way."

He heard the sarcasm in his voice and exhaled. This wasn't how he'd planned on talking. He wanted to be reasonable. Calm. But the paper he held in his hand had taken those intentions and blown them sky-high. It certainly told him where he ranked on her priority list.

"I never had a cold," she admitted.

"I know. I can tell a virus from a bout of crying. You've been avoiding me ever since."

"I can explain that. Please, why don't we go in and sit down. Let me get you a drink and—"

"Does it have anything to do with this?" he asked, holding up the paper.

Her eyes lit on the note in his hand, then slid over to meet his gaze. "Where did you get that?"

"Off your counter." He swallowed tightly. "Were you going to tell me, Mel? Have you already done it?"

She frowned. "Done what?"

He shook the note, hurt, angry, unsure of what to call the other emotions rattling through him right now. "This is the clinic, right?"

She nodded. "Yes, but—"

"And even after last time, after you turned down my offer, after we started seeing each other, for God's sake, you still went ahead? Again?" He shook his head. "I trusted you. I thought we had...that we were..."

He loved her. He'd offered to father the child she wanted so badly. He'd wooed her, for the love of Mike. And she'd left him out, shut him out, gone ahead with her original plan as if he was nothing. As if what they had meant nothing. As if they had absolutely no future together, but she hadn't felt it necessary to tell him.

He tossed the paper on the table and walked out of the kitchen.

"Hold on a minute, Coop." Her command stopped him halfway to her front door. "How dare you! How dare you come in here and make assumptions and proclamations. What exactly are you accusing me of?"

He turned back around. "Did you or did you not have an appointment at the clinic in Edmonton?"

She put her hands on her hips. "I did."

He let out a sound of frustration. "You're still bent on this asinine idea of using a sperm donor! Have you been planning this all along? Just amusing yourself with me? Heck, let's go out with Coop and have some good times, but it's never going anywhere because I have my own plans. Never let anyone too close! And whatever you do, never trust anyone again. You went ahead with another treatment like what we had meant nothing!"

"Wow." She looked at him, but she'd masked her emotions so completely that he couldn't tell what she was thinking or feeling. "Now I know exactly what you think of me, Coop. What was your plan, to come in here and fix me and solve all my problems? News flash. I can solve my own problems. I've been doing just fine on my own."

"Oh, no doubt," he answered. The TV chattered in the background, the sound rasping on his already frayed nerves. "You're one hundred percent capable, you are. It's all about you now. No one is ever going to hurt you again because you won't let them. You're so bent on control that heaven forbid there's a father in your child's life. Someone to love it and you, right? I can't live like that, Mel. I can't. I can love for only so long without getting anything back."

He grabbed his hat from the back of the chair and put it on his head. "I deserve better."

He paused in the doorway. "You could have at least been honest with me instead of playing games."

The door was just starting to swing shut again when she came through it. "Playing games? Believe me, Cooper Ford, this has been anything but a game!"

"Keep your voice down. The neighbors will hear you."

She scoffed. "Oh, like you've ever given a good damn about that."

He stood on her front step. "Let's just leave it, before we say something we'll both regret."

"Oh, you mean leave it now that you've had your say and I don't get mine? How convenient for you. You don't want to hear how you got it all wrong, do you? Let me tell you something, Coop. Being with you—taking a chance—came with a whole lot of built-in pressure. It's pretty hard to be breezy about a relationship when the other person confesses to being in love with you half your life. There's no halfway in. It's all the way or no way. The only choice I had was taking it slow."

"Funny, because you always seemed to have one foot out the door."

"That's right," she admitted. "I did. Because being with you was the single most terrifying thing to happen to me since walking in on my husband in bed with another woman."

"Great. I'm so glad that we're equating dating me to the horror that was the end of your marriage. That tells me a lot."

"You're deliberately misinterpreting. What are you so afraid of?"

"Me?" Their voices were raised now, and he knew he should lower his, but couldn't seem to find the ability. "That's your thing, not mine."

She came all the way out onto the porch. "I moved on when we were kids, and I never looked back, right? And now you're so afraid of not holding on to every piece of me that you're pushing me away. Finding something to blame. Mainly me. After all, if you leave me first, I don't get the chance to leave you."

He shook his head. "This is ridiculous. You're the one who blew me off. You were the one who refused to take a next step with us, who backed away from intimacy, who started making bogus excuses when I called. You're doing all the pushing away. You don't think I see? You're lonely, Mel. And if you have a baby you won't be lonely anymore, and won't have to risk your heart, either. Win-win for you."

Her face paled as his words struck their mark, and he almost wished he could take them back. Almost. For the sake of total honesty he was glad he'd put into words something that had been bothering him for some time now.

She pressed a hand to her chest as if wounded. "That's a terrible burden to put on a child."

"Yes," he said quietly. "It is."

"Look, let's leave the baby thing out of this for a moment. You're right. I took a step back. To think. To make some plans. But tonight? You're so scared this is the end that you're making sure it is. You're making sure you can walk away from here absolutely certain that it's my fault."

"I don't see how it can be anyone else's," he answered. "That paper..."

"You didn't even ask what that paper was about. You saw what you wanted to see, Coop."

"If it's not that, what the hell is it?"

She shook her head and suddenly looked very sad. "No. Not tonight. Not now. Maybe not ever. But definitely not now. I'm too damned angry with you."

"I don't understand." She was talking in riddles.

"Because you never asked! Please leave, Coop. I don't know what to think right now and

I don't want us to say more that we can't take back."

He looked at her and realized that it was really over. He'd just been fooling himself, seeing what he wanted to see because he'd loved her for so long. But he needed more. He needed someone who loved him as much as he loved her. He couldn't live his life waiting for crumbs of affection. She had to be all-in, meet him in the middle. Maybe he'd been right the day he'd sat outside her shop with a container full of cookies. Maybe what he really needed was to let her go. Maybe they had to go through all of this so he could finally let the dream of her go and move on with his life.

"Just answer me this." He had to know. It was the one question that burned, the one he couldn't come up with an answer to no matter how he turned it over in his mind. "What changed? One day we were planning to grab a bite at the diner and the next you're home in your pajamas crying and refusing to see me again."

She was quiet for such a long time that he felt the traitorous stirrings of hope in his chest. Her eyes glistened as she shook her head. "No. I'm sorry. I can't talk about this now."

He'd bided his time, done everything slowly and the way she wanted, but this time it was truly, truly over. He didn't want to be bitter, but bitterness blackened his heart, anyway. "I was right," he murmured. "I do deserve better. I can't go on giving all of myself and getting nothing back in return. I'm not your fallback when things don't work out, Melissa. It's not fair to either one of us, so maybe it's better for us both to leave it here."

He walked out to the truck on wooden legs, got in, turned the key, put the vehicle in gear and backed out of the drive as if he was on automatic pilot.

It was time he faced the truth. He couldn't carry their relationship all on his own. He needed a partner. And Melissa, with all her plans and lists, needed guarantees and absolutes before she'd risk her heart.

The trouble was, no one could offer guarantees, and he knew for sure that whoever did was a liar. Life didn't work that way. It took a little faith. He could try to make her happy, but unless she gave up this crazy idea of relying only on herself, they didn't stand a chance.

And maybe what hurt the most was realizing how little faith she actually had in him.

Melissa waited a few days. She needed that time to let the dust settle. To stop being angry at Coop's erroneous assumptions. To put what had happened in perspective, and to get up the nerve to go to see him.

She was terrified. The only thing to do now was bare her soul and tell him everything, if they were going to have a chance to be together. She'd spent a very long time feeling "leavable" and never wanted to put herself in that position again. But Coop had walked away anyway. And she could be hurt and she could be angry, but she'd spent too much time on those sorts of feelings. He had jumped to conclusions, but she understood why. He was right. She had always kept one foot out the door because she was scared. Just as she knew he'd lashed out because *he* was scared.

They could either leave things as they were or she could take the first step toward repairing the damage. There really was no choice. She was miserable without him. Everything had changed. Loving him would be a risk, but for the first time in her life, it was worth the potential consequences. She had to at least try.

And that first step was telling him the truth about her appointment in Edmonton.

She waited until a weeknight, when he was most likely to be at home at the Double C, and drove out there in the dark. Her fingers drummed on the steering wheel as she forced herself to observe the speed limit even though the short drive seemed to take forever. The pounding of her pulse intensified as she turned in the lane and saw his truck parked in front of his house. The porch light was on and as she pulled up next to his half-ton she noticed potted mums on his front step. She inhaled deeply and breathed out slowly. This was so Coop. He was so settled, so sure of himself. He knew what he wanted and where he belonged. Except when it came to her. She knew he wasn't sure of her at all, because she'd never given him a reason to be. It was time she finally set things right.

The slam of her car door sounded terribly loud in the quiet night. She stopped for a moment, gathering her wits, staring up at the stars. Even though it was long past twilight, she focused on one twinkling pinpoint of light and closed her eyes. *Please let him be the one,* she wished. It was nearly the same wish she'd had the night on the swings. But then she'd wished for a baby, and tonight she was wishing for something else entirely, something that had somehow become more important to her—a future. Tonight was all about Coop and trying to repair the damage to their relationship. *And please,* she added, *let me find the right words to fix this.*

When Coop answered the door, she lost her train of thought. All her practiced introductions flew clean out of her head now that he was before her. She just stood there, looking up at him, loving him so hard, scared to death and without any idea where to begin.

"Mel," he said quietly.

"Can we talk?" She managed that much without stuttering.

He shrugged. A barrier fell over his eyes, shutting her out, but he stepped aside. Knees shaking, she moved past him into the foyer of his house.

She lost her breath momentarily. His place was beautiful. It was all creamy walls and high ceilings and gleaming hardwood. Ahead of her, white-painted railings wound around a circular staircase leading to the second floor. She'd expected a smaller version of the main house, but she hadn't expected it to be this fancy. Not for a bachelor. How lonely this huge house must be for one person.

"You want a glass of wine?"

"If you have it, that would be nice." Maybe it would steady her shaky nerves. It would at least give her something to occupy her hands.

She followed him into the kitchen, still bundled in her wool jacket. It was only when he turned around with the glass of wine in his hand that he noticed. "Oh. Let me take your coat."

She shrugged it off and handed it to him, exchanging the coat for the glass. As they traded, his fingers brushed against hers. Sparks jolted up her arm at the very touch, and their eyes clashed. *Thank God,* she thought. Some things hadn't changed. It gave her hope.

Melissa had just spent days avoiding him, sorting through feelings, wanting to work through what was in her head. Ironically, the one person she'd wanted to talk to most to work things through was the one person she couldn't ask—him.

But he was here now, and all she wanted was to draw from his strength. To feel safe. She put her glass down, stepped forward and wound her arms around his ribs.

She needed to feel close to him. Needed nothing more complicated than a hug right now from the one person who always seemed to make things better. She closed her eyes and pressed the side of her face against the solid wall of his chest while his arms cautiously came around her, still holding her coat. "Hold me," she murmured into the soft cotton of his shirt. "Just for a minute."

His arms tightened and he rested his chin on top of her head.

A lump formed in her throat. It was going to be okay. It had to be. She would find the right words somehow, and he'd understand. It couldn't be too late.

But there was so much to say that she truly didn't know where to begin.

"Why'd you come here?" he asked.

She spread her hands over the warmth of his back. He felt so good. So right. She tilted her head just a bit and replied, "I needed my best friend. I've needed him for a very long time, but I shut him out."

Coop backed out of her embrace. "You know how I feel, Mel. I don't want to be just friends."

"That's not what I want, either. But right now I need my friend Cooper to listen to what I have to say. It's important."

"You're asking too much." He put her coat over a chair and then rested his hands on top of it. His face was all hard lines and uncompromising angles. "Mel, if you're coming to say you're pregnant…"

He looked so tortured that she instantly took pity on him. "I'm not pregnant," she said clearly. "That would be impossible."

His eyes met hers, the barrier stripped away

for a moment as he latched on to that one very significant word. "Impossible?"

She nodded. "Can we go sit down somewhere? This could take a while and right now it feels like we're in a standoff."

And down came the shutters again. "Of course. Let's go into the living room."

She grabbed her glass of wine and took a healthy sip before following him there. The room, vaulted with cathedral ceilings, featured a surprisingly large angled window that faced north. During the day there was surely a gorgeous view of the Double C pastures. A fire snapped and popped in a fireplace complete with stone flue. It was like something out of a magazine. Mel had known that the Double C was doing well. She'd had no idea it was this prosperous.

She sank into the cushions of the soft leather sofa and toyed with the bowl of her wineglass for a moment. Then she put it down and shifted so she was facing him. "When you found my appointment card, you thought I'd gone for another fertility treatment, didn't you?"

"You mean you didn't?"

She shook her head. "No. I didn't."

"But…"

She reached out and put her hand on his forearm. "What bothers me most about that moment was that I realized you really don't trust me. You honestly thought I would go ahead and do that even though we'd started seeing each other."

"It was a pretty strong statement about where you thought our future was going," he remarked, pulling his arm away. "Nowhere. If you saw a future with me, you wouldn't be looking to be carrying someone else's child. You had to know that I…"

"That you what?"

He looked away. "That I'd find that impossible to live with."

She'd hurt him. Badly. She got what he was saying. She'd given him hope and then, in his eyes, stripped it away. She knew how cruel it was to have hopes crushed. Even though she really hadn't, and certainly hadn't meant to, she knew the fault was partly hers, because she hadn't wanted to say the words in the middle of an argument. She'd wanted everything to be perfect…and because of it she'd ruined everything.

"I backed away from us without telling you why, so I can't blame you for making the wrong assumption. I wasn't ready to explain and I certainly didn't want to do it when we were arguing. So I waited a few days. Thought a lot."

"Planned it? Like you plan everything?"

She nodded. "I do plan things. It comes from being surprised and blindsided and never wanting that to happen again. And this time it also comes from being scared and not wanting to mess up the most important relationship in my life."

She sighed, gathering strength. "Coop, when everything went wrong with my marriage, the one person I wanted to turn to was you. You had always, always been there for me, only this time you weren't. I think you probably would have been if I'd asked, but I couldn't. You hurt me, you see. I felt so foolish that I hadn't seen what was right in front of my face. I even felt foolish in front of you. It seemed everyone knew what was going on but me. Poor innocent Melissa. I decided then and there that I wasn't going to rely on anyone again. Especially not you—even though I missed you like crazy. Coop, we've always had a special bond, even when I was married to someone else. I made so many mistakes. When you said you deserved better? Well, if I'm being completely honest, we all did. I know that Scott and I should never have married in the first place. I'm partly to blame. We didn't have the kind of marriage we should have, and when that happens, people stray."

"People should get out first and not cheat."

"Agreed. But I can't help but wonder if Scott wasn't a bit jealous of our friendship."

Coop nodded. "I know he was. He threw it in my face when I threatened to tell you."

"It was all wrong," she said quietly, "but the one thing we can't do is turn back the clock and fix our mistakes. Which brings me to a few days ago."

She reached out again and took his hand in hers. "I know what scared looks like, Coop. I know because I've been terrified of my feelings for you. Ever since we made peace you've been everywhere I go. First the housing project, then Thanksgiving, at church, in my life. Not only that, but I had to get used to the idea of what you said that day by the creek."

She gave her head a little shake. "When I was fifteen you were all I thought about. I tried not to pressure you, because we were friends, but I wanted so much more. It finally got to a point where I just had to let go. I valued your friendship too much to push you away by demanding something you didn't want. So finding out over ten years later that you finally felt the same way… This all could have ended so differently. Sometimes that's made me a bit angry, to be honest. So much pain could have been avoided.

But then I tell myself that maybe we weren't ready then. Maybe we were too young. Maybe we had things to learn before we could be together. The last thing I wanted to do was play with your feelings. I know what it's like to love someone who doesn't love you back. That's why I wanted to take it slow. I was unsure, and I didn't want either of us to get hurt."

"I tried to give you space...."

His voice was hoarse and she blinked against the stinging at the backs of her eyes. "You did. You did every single thing I asked. And I had so much thinking to do. I wasn't as sure as you. I'd been going in one direction with a goal in sight and suddenly the road map changed. I'd been thinking about trying to have a baby for so long that it felt scary and strange to put it on hold while we explored this thing. But that's what I did, Coop. I put it on hold. The appointment at the clinic was not to give it another try. And I'm also to blame for you thinking that. I pulled away from you without an explanation. It's not surprising that you jumped to the conclusion you did."

Coop's brows knitted together. "If things were going so great, then why did you pull away?"

Here it was, the moment of truth. "This is

so hard," she whispered. Once it was out she couldn't take it back. Things would change forever.

"Is there someone else, Mel?"

Her heart lurched as he asked it quietly, cautiously, as if preparing himself for the worst.

"No," she whispered, sliding over and lifting her other hand to his cheek. "No, Coop. There's no one but you, I promise."

No one but you.

And with her next words she was going to hand him so much power it was staggering.

"That night at the diner, when we were supposed to meet? I showed up," she began. "You were there, talking to Ty and Clara and there was a moment where you caught Susanna and lifted her in your arms. This little curly-haired doll in your big strong arms, Coop. She kissed your cheek and you kissed her hair. And that was the moment. It was like the world tilted and suddenly there was a brand-new reality in front of me. It wasn't just us seeing where things were going anymore. It hit me so hard. I love you, Coop."

"You love me."

She nodded, felt one tear slip down her cheek. Why did his voice sound so tight rather than happy? Why wasn't he pulling her into his arms and telling her it was okay? Panic started to slither through her veins, making her chest tight as she hurried to explain. "I realized I was in love with you, and I didn't know what to do with everything I was feeling. I had to make sense of it all. It scared me so much. I never wanted to care for someone that much. I've let go of you twice already, don't you see? And it hurt so badly both times. The idea of having to do that again someday—after sharing a life with you, after knowing what it is to have you—I'm not sure my heart could survive that. So I backed away, tried to make sense of my feelings. To decide what to do."

"And the appointment?"

He was still fixated on the clinic appointment. This wasn't going at all as she'd hoped. She'd thought she would say the words and it would make everything all right. That he'd confess his love, too, and she'd be in his arms by now. But Coop seemed more distant than ever. Maybe if he understood the reason behind the appointment he'd see the same future she envisioned in her heart.

"I've done a few treatments now and it hasn't worked. I was going for further testing to make sure there's not a fertility issue. For us. Just in case…"

Coop got up from the sofa and went to the window. What was his problem? She'd explained the appointment and just told him she loved him, and he was cold as ice!

"What's wrong?" she asked. "I thought once I explained the appointment, once I told you how I was feeling, you'd…"

"I'd what? Throw myself in your arms?"

Confused and afraid, she gave a quick nod. "Well…yes, something like that. Isn't that what you wanted?"

He cursed and ran his hand through his hair as he turned back to face her. "Yes, it's what I wanted! But it's not that easy. When your marriage broke up, the one thing you were trying to do was start a family. It's so important to you that you were prepared to make it happen all on your lonesome. Then I jump in and complicate the whole thing—especially when I made that stupid offer to help you. Oh, I wish I'd never done that…."

He started pacing in front of the fireplace. "Now you come to me and say you love me after…" He heaved a breath and stopped, facing her directly. "After you see me holding some kid, and decide I'd make perfect father material?"

"Don't you want children?" she asked, feeling desperately as if she was losing him, and not understanding why. "You'd be such a good father...."

"What I want," he said significantly, "is a woman who loves me for me and not my DNA."

She sat back on the sofa, her mouth hanging slightly open. Was that how he saw her? That she was so fixated on having a baby she couldn't tell the difference between love and a means to an end? Was he so unsure of her that he'd think she'd use him that way?

"What do you want me to say?" Mel asked weakly. "I can't lie and say I don't want children, because I do. Can you stand there and say you don't want a family, too? That doesn't mean I don't love you, Coop. I'm just not sure how to prove it to you."

"I'm not sure you can." His voice was flat and resigned.

There was a long pause where the only sound was the fire crackling. Finally Coop looked down at her. "I thought I knew what I wanted. I thought by telling you about my feelings at Thanksgiving, it would somehow work out. Believe me, no one is more surprised than me at what I'm saying right now. Everything I wanted is right in front of me and I'm not reaching out to take it."

"Why?"

"Because a part of me would always wonder if you were with me for me, or if I was just part of a plan you had for the perfect life."

She got up from the sofa. "I had a plan like that once. It didn't turn out so well. I try not to repeat the same mistakes. I thought that was why I was here. I don't know which is worse— the idea that you don't have faith in me to love you or the lack of faith you have in yourself to be able to hold me."

The future was slowly slipping out of her fingers, but she was glad she had come. She'd said the words and she'd meant them. She'd meant every syllable. She went to him and lifted her hand, brushed his hair back by his ear with her fingertips. "You're breaking my heart right now," she murmured.

"I can't be someone who is just *enough,*" he replied, stopping her hand by circling her wrist with strong fingers. "I can't be second best or an alternate choice. If we do this, I have to be *everything.*"

"You are everything," she replied, gazing deeply into his eyes. "That's what I'm offering, Coop. I love you. If you send me away tonight, that won't change. I was afraid of falling in love. Afraid to give anyone that much control over my life, because when you're in love you put that other person ahead of yourself." She moved closer so that their clothing brushed. "Loving you means handing you my heart for safekeeping. I get that now, because seeing you that night, I realized my heart was no longer mine to give."

She stood on tiptoe and touched his cheek with her lips. "It's you, Coop. It's always been you. And nothing you say or do will change that."

"What if your test results say you can't have children? What if, by some crazy circumstance, I can't? What then?"

She put her hand over his heart, feeling the strong beat against her palm. "I would be upset and disappointed. And I would hope that we would face it together. The day you made your offer to help, I told you that I didn't believe in marrying someone just to have a baby. I meant that with all my heart. I don't want your DNA, Coop. I want a *partner.* Someone who loves me for me and someone I adore in return. Someone I can talk to about anything and trust with my life. I want to put aside my dreams and replace them with *our* dreams. I can't imagine being with anyone but you."

"You really mean that, don't you?" he asked,

and she saw a tiny crack in the wall he'd built around himself. He put his hand over hers, his strong fingers circling her wrist once more.

She nodded. "I do," she confirmed. "The night you came to see me, you asked me what had changed. My whole world changed that night. Everything I thought I knew no longer existed. And if I needed time to plan, it's because the one thing I didn't want was to screw this up. So please, please. Trust me. Love me. Let this be everything."

For a long moment silence hummed between them. Coop seemed to struggle, and she thought that her one last effort to reach him was a failure. Then he loosened his grip on her wrist and his Adam's apple bobbed as he swallowed. "I'm so afraid," he admitted. "I thought I couldn't love you more than I already did, and then there you were, and it was more than I ever imagined. You have the power to hurt me, Mel. And I got so scared, because if love just gets bigger, then losing you would destroy me, and I could feel you slipping away."

"Then don't lose me," she replied. "I'm not going anywhere. I promise."

His dark eyes shone in the firelight. "Then stay," he commanded. "Stay with me tonight. We've wasted so much time already."

She knew what he was asking. There would be no turning back after this. And for the first time in years, there was no hesitation, no insecurity, no fear in not knowing exactly what the future would bring. Instead there was relief and happiness and a strange but welcome sense that everything in her life was finally right where it was meant to be. In this moment.

"Let's not waste any more," she replied.

CHAPTER TWELVE

GRILLING WAS COOP'S specialty, and despite the brisk day and snow clouds building to the west, he had a roaster full of ribs ready to slap on the barbecue. The playoffs had started and dinner was at his place today, and Mel had agreed to come over and help with the meal.

He came back in from the deck, where he'd turned on the barbecue to heat, and saw her standing at the threshold to the kitchen. The pre-game was on the television and the announcers' voices were muffled. She looked beautiful in faded jeans and his Eskimos jersey, which was about two sizes too big. Beautiful and adorable and his.

"You're early."

"Mmm-hmm." She put grocery bags down on the counter and walked over to him in stocking feet. "I wanted to get here before your parents."

"Really. And why is that?"

A slow smile curved her lips. "So I could do this without an audience."

She wrapped her arms around his neck and pressed her mouth to his. With a chuckle he blindly put the lighter on the counter and pulled her closer, cupping one hand around her neck as they kissed fully, completely.

"I don't suppose we have time..." she murmured, slightly out of breath.

"Why, Miss Stone," he teased. "Are you suggesting..."

She grinned. "Yeah, like you're surprised."

Being with Mel was more than Coop had ever dreamed. She was beautiful, responsive, loving. They'd been using protection at her insistence, so that he'd be absolutely sure of her and her motives. They needed to do this right and with total honesty, and when the time came...

Which was why he put his hands on her arms and pushed her away gently. Today he was going to be as honest as it was possible to be.

"I have something for you," he said, stepping aside and opening a drawer. He took out a flat, rectangular box that was wrapped in blue foil with a silver ribbon.

Her eyes lit up. "A present?"

He handed it over, hoping to God his fingers weren't shaking. "Open it."

It seemed to take forever for her to get through the ribbon and wrapping. She was very precise, careful not to rip anything, which was starting to drive him a little crazy. His parents would be here at any moment and he wanted her to himself just a little bit longer....

Her laugh bubbled out as she lifted the lid to the box. "Oh!" she exclaimed, reaching in. "Coop, this is so funny!"

She held up the canvas apron and slid the loop over her neck, laughing as she read the front. "'Keep Calm and Cowgirl Up.' Cute."

"I thought that if you're going to be hanging out with us Fords and helping with the cooking, you need your own apron."

"Thank you, Coop. I love it." She secured the ties around her waist and spun in a circle. "Now, about my first proposition…"

She wound her arms around him again and whispered a suggestion in his ear that made him go hot all over.

"Wait," he said hoarsely. As much as seeing her in that apron—and only that apron—was an intriguing idea, there was something more important that came first. "I noticed that your work apron at the shop has lots of pockets to keep stuff in."

With an impatient sigh she admitted, "I do love my pockets. They're very handy."

"This apron has pockets."

"So I see."

It was hard to think with her pressed so tightly against him. "Mel," he insisted, closing his eyes. "Maybe you should check the pockets."

He didn't know if it was something in his voice that did the trick, or the words themselves, but Mel stood back and met his gaze with wide eyes. And held it as she dipped her fingers into the wide pockets of the cobbler's apron.

He knew when she found the ring, because her eyes widened even further and started to glisten. She slowly took it out of the pocket and held it between two fingers. "Coop..."

He went to her and took the ring from her hand. "I love you, Mel. I've loved you for so long that it's hard to remember a time when I didn't. I tried, God knows I tried, when I thought there would never be a chance for us, but no one ever measured up to you. Now that you're mine I want to keep it that way. Forever."

She sniffled, and his chest expanded with emotion and possibility and hope and fear and a million other emotions.

"I want you to marry me. I want to make a life with you, and see you every morning when

I wake up, and hold you close every night when I go to sleep. I know you're scared and you want guarantees. Some guarantees are impossible to give because we don't know what life holds for us. But I can promise you this—I will love you until my dying breath. I will always be there for you. I want to have a family with you. I want everything from you and I'll give you everything I have in return. Will you marry me?"

Her lip quivered. "I love you, Coop. Yes, I'll marry you. Yes, yes, yes!"

It felt as if his heart was exploding with relief and happiness, even though it still beat along in his chest, perhaps just a tiny bit faster than normal. As she sniffled again, he held up her hand and slid the ring over her knuckle. The simple square-cut diamond caught the light and sparkled as he squeezed her fingers. He'd never thought this day would actually come. That she'd say yes. That he'd have everything he'd ever dreamed of having.

The front door opened, bringing a gust of wind tunneling through the foyer and into the kitchen. "Hello!" called Jean. "We're here!"

Coop cupped his hands around Mel's face and gave her a quick kiss during their last few moments of privacy. "I'll take a rain check on that other offer," he murmured with a secret smile.

* * *

When his parents entered the kitchen, Mel and Coop broke apart. She stayed in the shelter of his arms, though, wanting to remain close. They were going to do it. They were getting married. And one day they'd start a family together. It surprised her to realize she didn't want that to happen right away. She wanted a little time for just the two of them first.

"I see we're interrupting," Jean said, her eyes twinkling as she set a casserole dish on the countertop. Mel grinned at the approving note in her voice, and the sound of Bob's dry chuckle behind her.

"Not at all," Melissa replied, dropping her arms.

"Oh, look at you!" Jean laughed. "Nice apron."

"I figured if everyone else in the family had one, then Mel should, too," Coop said. "Especially since…"

He looked down at her and his dark eyes were filled with love and hope and happiness. "Especially since I asked her to join the family about five minutes ago."

Jean hurried around the corner of the counter. "You asked her to marry you?" To Mel's delight, Coop's mother grabbed her hand and lifted it to see the evidence. "Oh, Bob! Look! She has a ring and everything!"

"It's about time," was all Bob said, coming forward to clap Coop on the arm. Then he stopped to fold Mel into a hug. "Welcome home," he said softly, making more tears prick the backs of her eyes. "We've been hoping for this for a very long time."

She squeezed him back.

Jean interrupted the moment with a question. "Do your parents know?"

"Of course not. It just happened." Mel laughed. "But they're going to be very happy." She didn't mention their displeasure with her other recent decisions, but knew for sure that the news that she was marrying again—and marrying Coop—would be cause for celebration in the Stone household.

"Then get on the phone, girl! Invite them over. There's plenty of food and this deserves a party."

Bob went to work putting beer in the fridge, while Jean bustled around, taking stock of food supplies. Mel took advantage of the chaotic moment to snuggle close to Coop. "Sorry about the hoopla," she murmured. "Looks like that private celebration will have to wait."

"It's okay," he answered, dropping a sweet kiss on her forehead. "We've got all the time in the world. We've got forever."

* * * * *

COMING NEXT MONTH from Harlequin® Romance
AVAILABLE AUGUST 6, 2013

#4387 THE COWBOY SHE COULDN'T FORGET
Slater Sisters of Montana
Patricia Thayer

Ana Slater knows she can't look after her ranch alone. Her only hope is the cowboy she has found it impossible to forget—Vance Rivers.

#4388 A MARRIAGE MADE IN ITALY
Rebecca Winters

Leon Malatesta is fiercely protective of his baby daughter. But does Belle Peterson's arrival bring the possibility of a new future for all of them?

#4389 MIRACLE IN BELLAROO CREEK
Bellaroo Creek
Barbara Hannay

Ed Cavanaugh always knew Milla Brady deserved true love. So when he arrives in Bellaroo Creek, he resolves to tell her how he truly feels....

#4390 THE COURAGE TO SAY YES
Barbara Wallace

Abby Gray needs a fresh start to finally put the past behind her. Can Hunter Smith convince her that happy-ever-afters do happen in real life?

HRLPCNM0713

LARGER-PRINT BOOKS!

GET 2 FREE LARGER-PRINT NOVELS PLUS
2 FREE GIFTS!

♥HARLEQUIN®

Romance

From the Heart, For the Heart

YES! Please send me 2 FREE LARGER-PRINT Harlequin® Romance novels and my 2 FREE gifts (gifts are worth about $10). After receiving them, if I don't wish to receive any more books, I can return the shipping statement marked "cancel." If I don't cancel, I will receive 4 brand-new novels every month and be billed just $4.84 per book in the U.S. or $5.24 per book in Canada. That's a savings of at least 19% off the cover price! It's quite a bargain! Shipping and handling is just 50¢ per book in the U.S. and 75¢ per book in Canada.* I understand that accepting the 2 free books and gifts places me under no obligation to buy anything. I can always return a shipment and cancel at any time. Even if I never buy another book, the two free books and gifts are mine to keep forever.

119/319 HDN F43Y

Name _____ (PLEASE PRINT) _____

Address _____ Apt. # _____

City _____ State/Prov. _____ Zip/Postal Code _____

Signature (if under 18, a parent or guardian must sign)

Mail to the Harlequin® Reader Service:
IN U.S.A.: P.O. Box 1867, Buffalo, NY 14240-1867
IN CANADA: P.O. Box 609, Fort Erie, Ontario L2A 5X3
Want to try two free books from another line?
Call 1-800-873-8635 or visit www.ReaderService.com.

* Terms and prices subject to change without notice. Prices do not include applicable taxes. Sales tax applicable in N.Y. Canadian residents will be charged applicable taxes. Offer not valid in Quebec. This offer is limited to one order per household. Not valid for current subscribers to Harlequin Romance Larger-Print books. All orders subject to credit approval. Credit or debit balances in a customer's account(s) may be offset by any other outstanding balance owed by or to the customer. Please allow 4 to 6 weeks for delivery. Offer available while quantities last.

Your Privacy—The Harlequin® Reader Service is committed to protecting your privacy. Our Privacy Policy is available online at www.ReaderService.com or upon request from the Harlequin Reader Service.

We make a portion of our mailing list available to reputable third parties that offer products we believe may interest you. If you prefer that we not exchange your name with third parties, or if you wish to clarify or modify your communication preferences, please visit us at www.ReaderService.com/consumerchoice or write to us at Harlequin Reader Service Preference Service, P.O. Box 9062, Buffalo, NY 14269. Include your complete name and address.

HRLP13R

SPECIAL EXCERPT FROM

 HARLEQUIN®

Romance

*Don your Stetson and your cowboy boots as
Patricia Thayer brings you first loves, second
chances and happy-ever-afters in the*
SLATER SISTERS OF MONTANA *series.*

ANA NEVER WAS one to take risks. She was the oldest, the sensible daughter. She always tried to do the right thing. So why was she walking across the compound to Vance's house just before dawn? She was afraid to even answer that question. She was shaking as she walked up the steps, then before she could chicken out, she knocked on the door. She stood there a few minutes and almost felt relieved when there wasn't an answer. Just as she started to leave, the door opened and Vance stood there wearing only a pair of jeans and a towel draped around his neck.

Oh, God. She loved looking at this man. She met his eyes and tried desperately to speak, but nothing came out of her mouth.

He reached for her, pulled her into the house and closed the door, pushing her back against it. A soft light came from over the stove in the kitchen, letting her see the look of desire in his eyes.

"What are you doing here?"

"I didn't like how we left things last night."

"So you thought coming here just before dawn was a wise thing to do?"

"I couldn't sleep."

"Join the club, lady. You've kept invading my dreams ever since you've come back home."

His honesty shocked her. "Really?"

In answer, he lowered his head and covered her mouth with his. With a soft moan, she gripped his bare arms, feeling his strength. Yet he held her with tenderness as he placed teasing kisses against her lips.

"We could bring my dreams to life if you like," he told her before he gave her another sample. He captured her mouth in a deep kiss, causing her knees to give out.

He wrapped his arms around her, pulling her close. "I got you," he whispered.

She laid her head against his chest, feeling his rapid heartbeat. "I've always wanted you, Vance," she breathed.

THE COWBOY SHE COULDN'T FORGET
by Patricia Thayer is available August 2013 only from Harlequin® Romance.